"The man is middle-aged, leonine, rav-
aged. The girl is young, foxlike, insouciant.
Total strangers, they are inspecting an un-
furnished Paris apartment that is for rent.
Suddenly the man scoops the girl in his
arms, carries her to the side of the room.
He tears off her panties and has sex with
her while still dressed and standing. The
camera rests steadily on them as he thrusts
her against the wall and she hitches herself
up on him, clinging to his body with her
knees. Finally, gasping and groaning, they
tumble to the floor. . . . Any moviegoers
who are not shocked, titillated, disgusted,
fascinated, delighted or angered by this
early scene should be patient. There is
more to come. Much more."—*Time*

"A SEXUAL REALITY SUCH AS HAS
NEVER BEFORE BEEN SEEN!"
—*The Sunday Journal* (Paris)

An **ALBERTO GRIMALDI** Production

# Marlon Brando

in

# Last Tango in Paris

## A Film by Bernardo Bertolucci

with

# MARIA SCHNEIDER

MARIA MICHI · GIOVANNA GALLETTI

and with

# JEAN-PIERRE LEAUD

also starring

# MASSIMO GIROTTI

Produced by **ALBERTO GRIMALDI**

Directed by **BERNARDO BERTOLUCCI**

A Coproduction

PEA Produzioni Europee Associate S. A. S.—ROME

Les Productions Artistes Associes S. A.—PARIS

## UNITED ARTISTS

a novel by
ROBERT ALLEY

A DELL BOOK

in association with
QUICKSILVER BOOKS, INC.

*Published by*
*Dell Publishing Co., Inc.*
*1 Dag Hammarskjold Plaza*
*New York, New York 10017*
*and*
*Quicksilver Books, Inc.*
*200 West 54 Street, New York, N. Y. 10019*

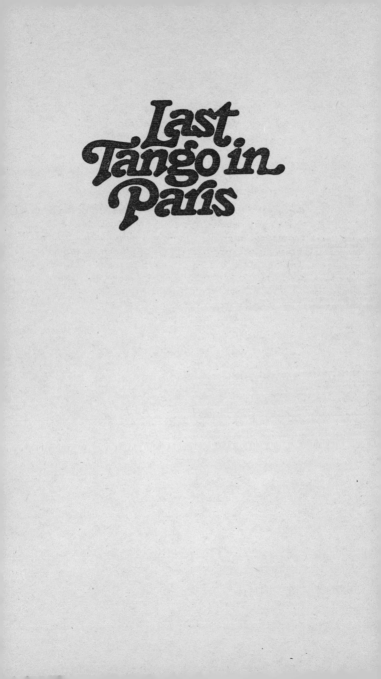

# Chapter One

DAZZLING winter sunlight played among the fluted arches of the ornate railway bridge, casting a latticework shadow over the dark waters of the Seine. Below the elevated Métro, along a walkway resembling the interior of some vast and sumptuous hall, pedestrians advanced and passed one another in silence, locked in a strange and compelling ritual. Flowering columns of blue-gray iron completed the illusion of an island of art nouveau, suspended in time. The distant January sun could add no warmth to the scene's splendid decline, violated by the earthy smell of the river, the reek of burned chestnuts drifting up from the quay, the shriek of punished metal as the train clattered overhead. The long lament of its whistle

7

marked the prelude of an exquisite and irrepressible concerto. The dance had begun.

Two people crossing the walkway, moving in the same direction, were already locked into this mutual cadence, though they did not suspect it, had never met, and could not have explained this curious conjunction of time and circumstance that had brought them together. To each of them the bridge, the day, the Paris skyline, and the conditions of their own existence meant something entirely different, or nothing at all, and any chance of an encounter would have seemed infinitesimal.

His profile was like that of a hawk, arrogant and uncompromising even in grief, for he was weeping as he aimlessly ambled from column to column. His body was thick and heavily muscled, and he moved with the physical carelessness of an aging athlete, running blunt fingers through his hair, shoving a workman's hands into the pockets of his camel's-hair overcoat, which was slightly soiled but well-cut in the style made notorious by certain American gangsters. His shirt was open, exposing a bullish neck.

"Fucking god!" His scream of anguish mingled with the clamor of a train passing overhead. At that moment his face, though unshaven and tormented, reflected an angular precision and a delicacy about the mouth and eyes that was almost feminine; at the same time, he seemed coarse, brutish. He was about forty-five years old, and handsome in a dissolute way. Other men confronting him in the shadow of the arches stepped aside.

The girl was half his age. She wore a soft brown felt hat at a rakish angle, and the impetuous expression of the young and the beautiful. Her walk was provocative to the point of impertinence; she swung her handbag on a long leather thong, wore a white suede maxicoat, and her face was set in a silver-fox collar. The lashes were lightly brushed with mascara, the full, pouty mouth carefully prepared with lipstick that appeared moist and fresh. The coat could not totally obscure her full, vigorous body, which seemed to have a will of its own.

Their names were Paul and Jeanne. For her, the smell of the Seine and the reflection of sunlight in the leaded bow windows of houses along the quay, the electrical flash beneath the belly of the Métro, and the appreciative glances of the men passing were an affirmation of her own existence. For him, these things meant nothing, even if observed, except that they were random manifestations of the physical world he detested.

She saw him first, and did not look away when he turned his distracted but unwavering eyes on hers: something happened in that first exchange. A man she assumed to be a derelict became suddenly remarkable, perhaps because of the tears and the contradictory sensation of suppressed violence. He saw only an object, one more sensually pleasing than most, but still an object tossed into the path of his own absurd wanderings.

Jeanne had the fleeting impulse to touch his moist, unshaven cheeks; Paul was surprised by a tug of lust, and wondered if the sensation could represent reality. For several seconds they walked abreast, locked in step, their expressions revealing nothing more than vague interest; then she moved ahead, as if he were an anchor attached to her by an invisible but irresistible thread. She reached the end of the bridge and passed out of the lush, *fin de siècle* ambience and into a harsh contemporary world, where automobile horns could not be construed as music, the blueness of the sky was too pure and too abrupt, and that irresistible thread snapped—or grew limp—and was momentarily forgotten.

She passed the Café Viaduc, on the Rue Jules Verne. The street was deserted, although it was morning rush hour and Paris was vibrant with traffic. She walked up the street until she reached a towering iron gate backed by opaque yellow glass. A hand-written sign taped above the bell read: "APARTMENT FOR RENT. FIFTH FLOOR." Jeanne stepped back, squinted up at the ornate balconies layered against the sky. She had discovered the apartment building by chance, and she wondered what sort of flat would be available behind the squat, thick, sensuous pillars, and the half-drawn shutters that gave the windows the look of somnolent, lecherous eyes. Jeanne had a fiancé, and she and Tom had spoken often of setting up house together—though these discussions were always general, almost academic—and it occurred to her that this might be the apartment to transform speculation into actuality.

She heard footsteps, and once glanced behind her, but the street remained empty. She walked back to the café. Workmen in overalls hunched over the polished aluminum bar, sipping strong coffee and cheap cognac before beginning their tasks. They appraised Jeanne as she swung through the door—the way men always did—but she ignored them and hurried down the stairs to the telephone.

The light in the booth burned at the end of the corridor. Before she could reach it, the door to the men's room opened, and Paul stepped out. She was surprised to see him, and oddly frightened, and she pressed her back against the wall to let him pass. He looked at her, was secretly gratified by their close proximity and the coincidence of the meeting. He felt the same basic, lustful impulse, and didn't bother to examine the subtler aspects of her face and her clothes, any more than he had when he chanced to observe her on the walkway under the bridge. It seemed supremely ironic that he would be distracted in his grief by something so banal as a pretty girl.

He passed her without so much as a smile of recognition, and left the café.

Jeanne was vaguely disturbed by the meeting: the inexplicable attraction she felt on the bridge had recurred, and she found it oddly humiliating. She stepped into the booth, deposited her *jeton,* and dialed, without bothering to close the door.

"Mamma," she said, "this is Jeanne. . . .

There's an apartment in Passy I'm going to see.
. . . Then I go to meet Tom at the station. . . .
See you later. . . . Kisses, so long."

She hung up and climbed the stairs. Outside,
the street seemed too bright for winter, preserved
in an aura of timelessness. A sleek black Citroën
eased past, but it was an exception; empty scaffolding seemed to support one of the elegant old buildings in the middle of the block. She paused for a
moment on the pavement, and felt the fresh flowers
pinned to the crown of her hat; she was pleasantly
aware that the men in the bar were watching her,
as she turned and sauntered back toward the apartment building.

She rang the bell and pushed open the heavy
iron door. Behind the opaque yellow glass was a
dimly lit foyer thick with the smells of Gauloise
cigarettes and something vaguely unpleasant bub-
bling on a stove somewhere upstairs. Light filtered
through high, unwashed windows illuminated the
elaborately wrought cage of the elevator; panels
of more opaque yellow glass separated the entrance
hall from the concierge's office, and Jeanne stepped
up to the tiny open window.

An obese black woman sat facing the opposite
wall, reading a newspaper. Jeanne cleared her
throat, to get the woman's attention, but she remained motionless and uninterested.

"I've come about the apartment," Jeanne said
finally. "I saw the sign."

The concierge turned her head, and Jeanne saw
that she had cataracts on both eyes.

"The sign?" the woman said, staring off hostilely toward a corner of her cubicle. "Well, nobody tells me nothing."

She began to hum—a tuneless utterance that sounded more like keening—and turned away again.

"I'd like to see it," Jeanne said.

"You want to rent it?"

"I don't know yet."

The woman heaved herself to her feet with what seemed like a tremendous effort. She began a litany of complaints.

"They rent. They sublet. They do what they want. And I'm the last person to know about it. Do you have a cigarette?"

Jeanne hoisted up her bag, took out a package of Gitanes, and passed them through the window. The concierge extracted a cigarette, after Jeanne quickly drew her hand away, reluctant for the woman to touch her. She lit her cigarette carefully, tilting her massive head in an effort to see the tip, and inhaled deeply. Instead of handing the package back, she dropped it into the pocket of her tattered sweater.

"Didn't used to be like that," she said. "Go up, if you want to. But you'll have to go alone. I'm afraid of the rats."

Her voice was immensely old. It was as if Jeanne was attempting to gain entrance to some shadowy and threatening netherworld, and the gatekeeper was bent on preventing her. This old woman, like Charon at the gates of Hades, demanded payment before admitting suppliants; Jeanne wondered if she would disappear in the depths of the building.

The concierge fumbled with the big keys crowding the board above her chair.

"Key's disappeared," she croaked. "Some funny things going on around here."

The door next to the elevator cage opened with a creak. Jeanne saw an emaciated hand emerge, gripping an empty bottle, and set it down clumsily on the tiles. The hand disappeared, and the door sighed shut.

"They guzzle six bottles a day," the woman said absently, as if the tenants were animals instead of people.

Jeanne turned to leave. The seediness of the building bothered her, but not as much as the sense of isolation—the feeling of being caught in a place out of time, where there were no real people doing the things real people did, just the deformed and the almost-dead.

"Wait," the concierge called. "Don't go away. There's bound to be a duplicate."

She rummaged through a drawer and produced an old brass key.

"There it is," she said, and handed it to Jeanne, who recoiled from her soft, pudgy touch. But before she could withdraw her hand, the woman grabbed it in her own, and squeezed. An imbecilic smile revealed her dark, carious teeth.

"You're young," she cackled, rubbing her fingers over Jeanne's hand and wrist.

She jerked her hand away and walked to the

elevator. The woman was still cackling as Jeanne slammed the door of the cage; the old motor sighed as she began to ascend. The building reminded her of a mausoleum, grand in concept and construction, whose occupants could never be equal to its majesty, and allowed it to go into decline. There was no sound other than that of the old elevator, and the clash of the gate as she stepped out on the fifth floor.

The apartment door was broad and heavy, the lacquered wood almost black in the shadow of the elevator shaft. The grooved brass knob was shiny with the touch of many hands. Jeanne unlocked the door and let it swing open into the entrance hall. Immediately she was struck by the apartment's expansiveness and grace. Black-and-white tiles covered the floor of the hall; the paneling was in the same dark, sumptuous wood as that of the door. She moved respectfully, almost fearfully, into the corridor. She could see the beautiful detail of the parquet floor in the living room, and the soft yellow walls the texture of old parchment. The tall, curved panes of the bow windows, unwashed for a long time, diffused the sunlight that filled the room with the glow of burned gold. The room was a perfect circle. The egg-and-dart motif of the molding was broken just above the windows, a neat space of no more than a meter, where the plaster had fallen years before. Water marks scored the soft golden walls, and massive rectangular and oval paintings since removed left dark impressions like the shadows of departed tenants. The ambience was of elegant decline, rich and slightly decadent. Jeanne was both attracted by the sensual extravagance of the flat and repelled by the feeling of decay and the almost imperceptible odor of mustiness, which she associated with death.

She stepped into the circular living room and swept off her hat. She shook free her thick auburn hair that had been captive and performed a pirouette in the middle of the floor, but slowly, eyes and hands raised in appreciation. The light from the half-shuttered windows dazzled her; the shadows seemed to creep closer.

Suddenly she saw him. He was perched on the radiator, his head resting on his knees. She screamed and bit her fist. He didn't move.

"Who are you?" she gasped. She struggled to gain her composure, and backed slowly toward the door. "You frightened me," she said, as calmly as possible. Then she saw that he was the man from the bridge. "How did you get in?"

"By the door."

His voice was deep and vibrant. He spoke French with a foreign accent, with harshness and apparent contempt for the language.

Jeanne stood in the entrance to the corridor. Paul had not left his perch; all she had to do was turn and leave, but for some reason she hesitated.

"I'm such a fool," she said. "I left the door open. But I didn't hear you come in."

"I was already here." There was something sinister in his voice.

Jeanne turned and looked at his profile again. Her curiosity was aroused.

"I beg your pardon?" she said. Her question was irrelevant and received no response.

Paul's silhouette lengthened and broadened. His massive shoulders seemed fitted to the room's generous proportions, and he moved across the floor with a kind of heavy grace. His eyes were intelligent, very intense, and he looked at her mockingly, holding up another key clamped between thick fingers.

"Ah, the key," she said. "So you're the one who took it. . . ."

"She gave it to me," he corrected, still mocking her. Her obvious anxiety seemed petty to him, almost laughable. It made little difference to him whether she believed him or not, whether she stayed or whether she left, but he found her confusion amusing.

"I had to bribe the concierge," Jeanne said, and was surprised at her willingness to make conversation. Why didn't she just walk away from this strange man, who wept on the bridge and then hovered in the shadows of the empty flat? She wondered if he was insane.

"You have an American accent," she told him, as if perhaps he hadn't been aware of the fact; then she felt foolish.

Paul ignored her. He turned and paced regally about the room, inspecting the floors, where the wax had long since worn away, and the peeling walls, with an air of authority; he seemed as vain as he was strong.

"These old buildings fascinate me," said Jeanne.

"They're not too expensive for renting," he said condescendingly, and ran one finger along the mantelpiece. He paused and stared at the dust collected there, remembering the shock of seeing his dead wife, the way he had fled from their hotel after the police arrived, the look of fear on the faces of the other tenants. He couldn't remember what happened then. The face of the girl on the bridge seemed to bring his grief into focus, for she was so alive.

"An armchair would look good near the fireplace," Jeanne said.

"No," he contradicted. "The armchair has to go in front of the window." It was a command.

She kept herself at a distance from him, though she would have liked to look at him more closely, to inspect his clothes and the pale gray eyes almost hidden beneath a haughty, overriding brow. She could not understand why she welcomed his rebukes, and felt a strong desire to soften him.

They continued to inspect the room, and then moved into adjoining chambers, each committed to the pretense that they were interested in the flat itself, rather than in their unlikely meeting and the promise—or the threat—of its conclusion. They passed ceremoniously into the dining room, he a few paces behind her. Stacks of bound and yellowed newspapers lined one wall; an old bureau rested on three legs, and a jumble of broken crates and chairs and other furniture loomed beneath a filthy sheet. Paul attempted to balance the old bureau, and became preoccupied with obtaining an unsteady equilibrium, while he waited for the girl's reaction. He sensed her attraction and her fear, and decided that he would do absolutely nothing to assist her. It made no difference to Paul what happened, for he saw himself and her as two ridiculous bodies, without motive or consequence.

He closed his eyes and stifled the memory of the night before. When he opened them again, he saw that Jeanne had unbuttoned her coat, revealing a brief yellow skirt and legs that seemed abnormally long, lost in the embrace of soft calfskin boots. Her thighs were strong and inviting below the edge of the miniskirt. Her skin was firm, and seemed to glow in the refracted light. Paul could see that her breasts were large, and without need of the support of a bra. Jeanne threw her shoulders back.

"Are you going to rent it?" she asked.

"What about you?" His voice was husky now.

"I don't know."

Paul crossed the room to the windows. The tin and slate rooftops of Passy stretched away toward the river, a sea of crazy angular planes brushed a light blue-gray; the Eiffel Tower rose in the distance, spiny and erect, like a huge antenna draining energy from the sky. Both he and Jeanne stared at the tower, she impressed by its magnitude, and he by its pretension. Then Paul caught her reflection in the pane, and studied her body again. His stomach tightened, and his mouth grew dry.

She was intensely aware of his eyes upon her, felt both embarrassment and a kind of elation, as if she enjoyed his small humiliations of her.

"I wonder who lived here?" she said. "It's been empty for a long time."

She stepped out into the corridor and walked back toward the bathroom. She thought he would follow, but she heard his footsteps moving in the direction of the kitchen. Absently she inspected the bathroom, acutely aware of his movements at the far end of the apartment. The skylight over the tub bathed the room in light. The fittings of the double antique sinks matched the frame of the oval mirror. Jeanne paused to pat her hair and to glance at her makeup in the mirror. Then in a sudden daring moment she pulled down her underpants, raised her coat and skirt, and sat on the toilet. She knew it was an outrageous thing to do without locking or even closing the door, that he might walk into the room at any moment, and yet that possibility exhilarated her. She was terrified that he might find her there, and at the same time she hoped that he would.

Paul leaned against the wall in the kitchen and looked up at the pipes. The sound of the toilet flushing in the bathroom distracted and aroused him. Jeanne entered the kitchen, and they avoided each other's eyes, passing one another and entering separate rooms. Both realized that by prolonging the inspection, they increased the possibility of a confrontation. Neither of them actively wanted or sought this confrontation, and yet neither was willing to break out of the pattern. It was as if they had been choreographed and were reluctant to shatter the mood of the piece, or the aura of destiny contained within those walls.

The ring of a telephone was an unwelcome intrusion. Jeanne picked up the receiver in the bedroom, at the same time Paul answered the phone in the dining room. The strange voice of the caller trailed off, and he hung up, but Paul and Jeanne continued to listen, each intent on the other's breathing. She wished that he would speak to her, that he would make some small concession—some show of weakness—so that then she might be able just to stand and leave. Jeanne could not even hang up the phone, though she longed to slam it down on the ornate, antique carriage. It was his unyielding arrogance that held her. Perhaps Paul suspected this, for he was proud of his power.

He quietly placed the receiver on the floor, stood, and walked quickly across the circular living room and into the corridor. He could see her kneeling on the floor, her back to him, still listening. In the sunlight her hair shone bright orange, as if it were burning; she held her coat back with her other hand, and for a moment he studied the taut muscles of her thighs.

He moved quietly forward, and he glimpsed the expression of a child in anticipation, as Jeanne unconsciously ran the tip of her tongue across her lip. Then she saw him. She quickly hung up, in confusion and fright; she couldn't look at him. In that moment she both feared and hated him.

"Well, have you decided?" she asked, and she couldn't hide the resentment in her voice. "Are you renting it?"

"Yes. It was already decided."

His power had been affirmed, and he relented.

"Now I don't know," he said. "Do you like it?"

He took her hand, to help her stand. Her fingers were cool, smooth, and yielding, encircling his own; she felt the potential strength in his broad palm, and in the fingers once callused in some long manual labor. It was the first time they had touched, and their hands lingered. She had never felt so vulnerable.

"Do you like it?" he repeated, as their hands fell apart. "The apartment?"

"I have to think about it," she said anxiously. It was difficult to think about anything.

"Think fast," he said, using a slang expression that, in his mouth, sounded like a threat.

He left her. Jeanne heard the sounds of his footsteps in the corridor, the slamming of the front door, then nothing but her own breathing. A car horn blew briefly two blocks over, followed by complete silence. He's gone, she decided, and she felt suddenly drained. She picked up her hat from the floor and walked back through to the living room on the way out, deep in thought. Startled, she looked up. Paul was waiting for her, leaning against the wall. He seemed even bigger in the direct light of the sun, his chin raised and eyes veiled by half-closed lids. His arms were crossed on his chest; his overcoat hung open, revealing a thick, muscular torso and legs.

Jeanne said, "I thought you left."

"I locked the door." He walked slowly toward her, watching her wide, liquid-blue eyes, which reflected more resignation than fear. "Was I wrong?"

"No, no," she said, trying to catch her breath. "I just thought you were gone." Her words hung like an invitation.

Paul was at her in a second. He took her face in his hands and kissed her full on the lips. In confusion, she dropped her hat and her bag, and placed her hands on his broad shoulders. For a moment they stood absolutely still. Nothing in the circular room moved except the dust motes drifting in the sunlight; no sound reached them but that of their own labored breath. They seemed suspended in time, as did the faded beauty of the room, isolated from the world and their own separate lives. The room warmed and contained them in this brief, silent courtship.

Suddenly Paul swept her up in his arms and carried her across to the wall by the window, as effortlessly as if she were a baby. She put her arms around his neck, which felt as solid as a stump, caressed the muscles of his back beneath the smooth material of his coat. He had about him a slightly musty odor that was part sweat and something else she could not identify, which was more masculine than that of any young man she had known, and it greatly excited her. He set her down, but his powerful hands did not release her, pulling her to him and stroking her pendulous breasts through the material of her dress. This he unbuttoned with speed and adeptness, and slipped both hands inside, cradling her; he outlined her nipples with his thumbs. The toughness of his skin aroused her, and she thrust against him.

As if by prearrangement, they began to tear at each other's clothes. She gripped him through his trousers; Paul reached beneath her skirt, gathered the top of her underpants in his fist, and tore them away. Jeanne gasped at his audacity, clung to him in fear and anticipation. He eased one hand between her legs and lifted her almost off the ground; with the other he wrenched open his pants. Grasping her buttocks in both hands, he lifted her to him, and impaled her.

They clawed at each other like animals. Jeanne climbed the trunk of his body, gripping his hips with her knees, clinging to his neck like a lost child. He pressed her against the wall and drove deeper into her; for a moment they struggled awkwardly, as if in combat, but soon reached accord and began to labor in concert. Their bodies advanced and retreated like components in the most intimate of dances. The rhythm grew more frenzied, the music and the world forgotten, and they heaved and gasped, and beat themselves against the wall protecting that passion, and slipped beyond the origins of their own endeavor, dying gradually and without remorse on the tattered orange rug.

They lay motionless on the floor, without touching, their breathing gradually subsiding. Then Jeanne rolled away from him, cradled her head on her arm, looked up at the sky. Minutes passed, and neither spoke.

They stood and rearranged their clothes, their backs to each other. Jeanne set her hat at the same angle as before, and preceded him down the corridor and out onto the landing. Paul locked the door behind them; Jeanne buzzed for the elevator and turned modestly away from Paul. Minutes before, they had shared the most carnal embrace, and now, beyond the confines of the apartment, they were as distant as strangers.

She was grateful when Paul turned and walked down the stairs instead of joining her in the elevator. But they could not avoid meeting again in the foyer. She wondered what he might do next, walking just behind her as they passed the concierge's window, closed tight, and approached the door.

She preceded him into the street. The sunlight blinded them, and the sounds of Paris rang discordantly. Paul tore the hand-written FOR RENT sign from the door, crushed it, and tossed it into the gutter. For a moment they hesitated; then they turned in opposite directions, and neither of them looked back.

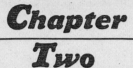

# Chapter Two

IT HAD happened so abruptly, it could have been rape, except Jeanne knew differently. She could still smell him, and feel the solidity of his body, but she experienced only exhilaration and bemused disbelief. It seemed incongruous that she could open herself completely to a total stranger, gladly receiving his semen and his violence, and then afterward go to meet another man whom she professed to love, and tell him nothing. The contradiction appealed to her.

The Gare St. Lazare was crowded. The vast dome resounded with the blasts of steam under pressure, and the ragged echo of a thousand feet shuffling along the railway platforms. All about her was movement and noise—a harsh reality—where earlier she had experienced a kind of suspension in time and the fulfillment of a romantic fantasy.

Jeanne purchased a pass at the ticket window and started down the platform. She moved against the force of the crowd, expecting to see Tom's face. She wondered if she might somehow appear changed to him. Friends often spoke of his superior perception. That worried her slightly, though it seemed that in the enormity of the crowd she was safe with her secret.

She stood on tiptoe, trying to spot Tom, and failed to notice that a young man in a denim jacket had crept up behind her and started filming with a black hand-held Arriflex camera. Next to the cameraman squatted a gaunt figure wearing headphones and carrying a Nagra tape recorder attached to a strap over his shoulder. He held a shotgun microphone in one hand, and he directed the tip of it first in one direction, then in another, picking up background noise. A script girl hovered behind both of them, gripping a sheaf of papers. Other passengers and those waiting for them paused to stare at the film crew, but Jeanne, looking for Tom, was oblivious to their presence.

Finally she spotted him. He wore a short leather jacket with a fur collar, a bright green-and-yellow ascot, and flared trousers. He looked younger than his twenty-five years, his dark hair carefully combed and trimmed, his gait bouncy and uninhibited, his smile as open and as innocent as a little boy's.

Jeanne pushed her way through the crowd and

threw herself into his arms. For a moment his embrace seemed tentative, even brotherly, compared with the unyielding trap of Paul's arms and shoulders. Just then the train beside them eased backward with a hiss of steam. As she pivoted to avoid the blast, she caught sight of the camera crew.

Surprised, she pulled back from Tom. "Do they take us for someone else, or what?" she asked, obviously annoyed.

Tom confronted the camera with a proud smile. He was first and last a filmmaker, a worthy student of Truffaut and Godard, and at the heart of his documentary method—*cinema vérité,* the French called it—was a devotion to spontaneity and concealment, even to the point of deception. Truth for Tom existed within the confines of sixteen millimeters of celluloid, screened at twenty-four frames a second. He was a sophisticated *voyeur,* who preferred to embrace life through the lens of a camera. In that way, he was the very antithesis of Paul.

"This is cinema," he said, "and that is my crew. We're making a film."

He lightly brushed Jeanne's lips with his own; there was something mischievous in the gesture.

"If I kiss you, that might be cinema."

He touched her hair.

"If I caress you, *that* might be cinema."

Inspired, he began to ascend the tenuous structure of his own vision. Jeanne pulled him back to earth.

"Stop it!" she demanded, waving her arms and expecting the camera crew to disappear.

"I know them," Tom protested. "I told you."

As if that answer was sufficient, Tom picked up his suitcase and escorted Jeanne toward the end of the platform. The crew moved with them.

"Look," he said, "I'm shooting a film for television. It's called 'Portrait of a Girl,' and the girl is you."

"You should have asked my permission."

The soundman crept forward, thrusting the long mike toward Jeanne.

"Yes," Tom said, though he was disappointed that she failed to appreciate his inventiveness. "I suppose it amuses me to begin with the girl of the portrait arriving at the station to meet her fiancé."

"And so you kiss me, knowing it's a film. Coward!"

In his preoccupation with filmmaking, Tom simply interpreted her anger as proof of her ingenuousness. Gently, he stroked her cheek.

"Most of all, it's a love story," he said. "You'll see."

The camera kept rolling.

"Now, tell me, Jeanne," Tom went on, "what did you do while I was away?"

Without giving it a second thought, she said, "I thought about you night and day, and I cried, 'Darling, I can't live without you.' "

The moment was electric. As sarcasm is lost on fools and children, so too was it lost on Tom. For him, Jeanne had at last assumed the role he envisioned for her, and he was radiant. Her performance thrilled him.

"*Magnifique!*" he shouted, gesturing to the cameraman. "That was perfect. Cut!"

# Chapter
## Three

NOT FAR from the Gare St. Lazare, on a narrow back street still paved with cobblestones, where two cars passed each other with difficulty and a visitor would be as likely to hear Italian or English spoken as he would French, stood several *pensions* that catered to transients. These little hotels had their complement of regular tenants—faded intellectuals and painters, failed actors, the occasional prostitute—and filled their other rooms with travelers and members of the seedier demimonde of Paris, including army deserters, drug addicts, pimps, and petty criminals. A tenuous bond existed among all these disparate types, since they all shared some degree of failure, and a common locale. The smell of garbage and old wine gone to vinegar, the clatter of the Métro at the nearby elevated station of Bir Hakeim, and the raucous noise from the corner bar, the proximity of furtive, illegal behavior—these were common to most residents on the street, as were hard, narrow beds, one barely respectable meal a day, and the desire for clear weather.

Paul had lived on the street for five years, in just such a *pension*, owned by the woman he had married. Her suicide meant the hotel was now his, though the prospect held little joy for him, since he despised the hotel and everything it represented.

For several hours after returning from the Rue Jules Verne, he put off visiting the room where his wife had killed herself. But by lunchtime, the maid had not yet come down, and Paul, curious, climbed the worn carpet covering the stairs. The wail of a saxophone carried throughout the hotel, emanating from a room on the far side of the courtyard, where a black Algerian and his wife lived in relative contentment. The Algerian, a self-taught musician, played the horn at all hours, but Paul had never asked him to stop, not because he enjoyed the music, but because it seemed no more objectionable than street sounds and the complaints of his tenants. The sound of it was both sensual and immensely sad. It also seemed quite futile to Paul.

On the third floor Paul pushed open one of the anonymous doors, and immediately confronted what looked like the scene of a massacre. Blood seemed to be everywhere—it had been splattered across the tiles of the bath area, streaked the shower

curtain trailing over the edge of the tub, and freck-
led the mirror above the sink. It looked as if several
people could have been bludgeoned to death there,
such was the bloody violence the room conveyed.

Paul was seized by nausea and anger. Without
speaking, he crossed the room and stood at the
window, waiting for the maid to finish cleaning the
tub. He wanted to cry, but couldn't: he was numb.
He had no idea why his wife had done it, and that
fact made his grief more absurd and more lonely.
Perhaps there was no reason, except to baffle him.

The faucet ran wide open. The maid dumped a
bucket of diluted blood down the drain, then
straightened and stared dumbly at Paul.

Paul gazed across the courtyard and into the
room where the Algerian continued to play his
tenor sax. The man's cheeks were distended, and
his muscular forearms bulged as he gripped the
keys and raised the horn above his head. His wife
knelt before him, patiently sewing a button on the
front of his trousers. When she finished, she bit off
the thread with her teeth, bringing her mouth
close to his groin. The simple intimacy of the act
escaped Paul.

"I wanted to clean up," the maid said, "but the
police wouldn't let me. They didn't believe in suicide—too much blood all over."

She tossed the bloody rag into a corner and
picked up another. Then she knelt and began to
wipe the tiles.

"They had fun making me reenact," she said, and
mimicked the cops' voices. " 'She went there. . . .

She went here. . . . She opened the curtain.' I did everything like her." She paused to scrape at a bit of dried blood with her fingernail. "The clients were awake all night, the hotel full of police. They played around with the blood. All spies!"

Paul looked around. The tarnished brass bedstead, the scarred wardrobe closet, the tattered screen decorated with Oriental versions of birds in flight—it was typical of every third-rate hotel in France, and yet Rosa had chosen the scene for her end. The room smelled of death even before her suicide.

The maid tossed her rag into a bucket half-filled with more diluted blood. She began to wash the shower curtain.

"They wanted to know if she was sad. If she was happy. If you fought, if you hit each other. And then, when you were married. Why you didn't have children. Pigs! They treated me like dirt."

Her voice was empty of emotion. Paul knew she and the other employees didn't like Rosa, because she took a genuine interest in their petty lives, and they came to expect more than they deserved.

The maid went on, "Then they said, 'Nervous type, your boss. You know he was a boxer?' So? Then he was an actor, then a bongo player. A revolutionary in Mexico, a journalist in Japan. One day he debarks in Tahiti, wanders around, learns French . . .'"

It was a list of accomplishments that he had once been proud of, but in the last few years had begun to view as meaningless. Rosa might have changed all that.

"Then he arrives in Paris." The maid continued her report. "And here he meets a woman with money, and marries her. 'Now what's your boss do? He's kept.' " She shrugged, never looking up from her work. "And I say, 'Can I clean up now?' And they say, 'Don't touch anything. You really think she killed herself?' "

She stood and dried her hands in her apron.

"And then he pushed me in a corner, trying to—"

"Why don't you turn off the water?" Paul interrupted.

She pushed greasy strands of hair from her forehead, leaned over, and shut off the faucet abruptly.

"Now it's all right," she said, surveying the room as if she had done nothing more than clean up after some unruly guest. "You can't see anything."

Paul turned and stared at the large, empty valise lying on the bed. It had contained Rosa's keepsakes, an odd collection of letters and photographs and little mementos—even a priest's collar, which he could not explain. All of it he had hidden from the police, not because he was afraid for them to examine the contents, but because he wanted to deny them that pleasure. The keepsakes had not given him any clues as to why Rosa killed herself, had not even seemed associated with her. He thought he knew his wife, that he had finally established lasting contact with another human being, but he was wrong. Paul's life had been a succession of romantic indulgence in doomed affairs; all his commitments to others—as hazardous as they were—had amounted to zero. When he was a young man, it didn't seem to matter, but he had recently come to realize that he would not live forever, and his death would be a solitary affair.

"What did they say about the suitcase?" he asked.

"They didn't believe it was empty. That's their tough luck."

Casually the maid took an old-fashioned straight razor from the pocket of her apron and handed it to Paul.

"Here's your razor," she said.

"It's not mine."

"They don't need it anymore. The inquiry is over."

Paul ran his thumb over the cold, blunt edge and felt the smooth bone handle. It was the instrument Rosa had ended her life with, and he was not going to surrender it.

"They told me to return it to you," she said, and watched for his reaction.

Paul dropped the razor into his jacket pocket.

"Put the suitcase away," he told her.

She moved to obey him. "There were so many slashes on her neck."

Paul cut her short.

"They'll do an autopsy," he said, and left the room.

The mood of the saxophonist had changed. The deep, sonorous melody was more sensual than melancholy, and Paul's thoughts turned to the girl and the events of the morning. The idea of sex without love, devoid of emotion, appealed to his morbid state of mind. It was a way to warm himself, however briefly, against the poverty of human desire and the certainty of death. There had been extra furniture stored in the basement, and he had already arranged for its delivery. The idea of making certain conventional concessions appealed to him. By placing a few miserable sticks of furniture in the apartment on the Rue Jules Verne, he would establish his presence.

Paul went directly down the stairs of the hotel and out the door, barely pausing to pick up his overcoat. There was always the chance that the girl would not return to the apartment, but he never considered it.

# Chapter
# Four

JEANNE ascended in the elevator, without really knowing why. The old contraption wheezed and sighed and threatened never to make it to the fifth floor. One part of her wished it would return to the airless foyer, which was still empty and offered only a view of the mad concierge, sitting with her back to her tiny window, humming tunelessly. Jeanne had tried to convince herself that she really planned to rent the apartment, on the chance that the man she'd met there hadn't actually taken it. But it wasn't the apartment she wanted now.

She rang the bell, then rang it again almost immediately. Nothing moved within that time-locked vault that she pictured in autumnal hues of muted red and gold. She gripped the key so tightly that her palm perspired.

A door opened on the floor above, followed by the sound of footsteps. Jeanne was seized by sudden, unreasonable panic. She didn't know what she feared more: being seen or being chased from the threshold of her adventure. In a single, impetuous moment, she inserted the key in the lock, turned it, and pushed the door open. The apartment embraced her; she felt at home. Quickly she closed the door, without even glancing behind her.

Jeanne turned and faced the narrow corridor connecting the several rooms, and moved slowly forward. Everything was as she remembered it. The sun had shifted, burnishing the opposing wall of the circular room. In the soft illumination, the water marks and cracks in the heavy wallpaper resembled the fine lines of a cardiogram. The excitement and the disbelief she had experienced that morning returned. That visit left her primed; she couldn't stop thinking about it, even while she was being filmed by Tom. She didn't know what to expect next.

Something moved. Jeanne wheeled around and saw in the corner next to the radiator a burly yellow cat, crouched in the shadow, watching her. She stamped her feet and advanced on the cat, hissing as if she were its rival. She resented the animal's intrusion and its blatant appraisal of her. The cat bounded up onto the windowsill and disappeared through the crack of the window left open. She pursued it even then, but found herself looking out over the rooftops, confronted by the distant spiny thrust of the Eiffel Tower, mocking in its massive permanence. The klaxon of a police car carried over to her from the far side of the Seine, and subsided. Once again the apartment assumed the air of a haven.

*"Allo!"* a voice called from the corridor.

For a moment the panic Jeanne had felt earlier returned. She raised the key and held it before her like a shield.

She expected a stocky man in a camel's-hair overcoat. Instead, she saw the legs of an armchair emerge from the corridor, supported by a pair of human legs in faded blue overalls and worn shoes. The chair descended, revealing a workman in a battered beret. A Gauloise dangled from his lips.

"All right, lady," he said with a thick Marseilles accent, "where do I put it?"

Jeanne was too surprised to speak. He walked to the center of the room without waiting for an answer, and set down the chair.

"You might have rung," she said, feeling extremely foolish.

"The door was open."

The workman detached the cigarette from his lips and trailed smoke from each nostril. The tip was stained dark brown with his saliva. "Can I put it here?" he asked, indicating the chair.

"No. In front of the fireplace." Jeanne was emphatic.

He scowled, moved the chair, and stalked out of the room. Jeanne decided that she, too, would leave. But as she went to the door, she was confronted by a second mover, dragging other chairs behind him.

"The chairs?" he asked her, and without waiting for an answer, he began to arrange them in a circle in the middle of the room.

The first mover returned with a table, which was circular and made of stained cherrywood, with a heavy scarred base. It didn't match the chairs—fake Windsors of some lighter wood, probably ash—and Jeanne wondered if the furniture belonged to the American. It seemed to Jeanne, who sold antiques, an odd lot for a man to assemble, though she could never have known that it was furniture taken from various rooms of an old hotel.

"What about the table?" the mover asked.

"I don't know," Jeanne said, pretending that she belonged there. "He'll decide."

The intrusion of the movers spoiled Jeanne's mood. Now she was certain someone else had rented the apartment. Again she started for the corridor, intent upon leaving; again she was blocked, this time by the workmen struggling under the weight of a double mattress. They unloaded their burden in a diminutive room off the corridor, though the mattress protruded through the doorway.

She handed them each a five-franc note as they left.

Now she was free to escape. But it was too late. The snap of the lock was sudden and harsh. She peered down the corridor and saw Paul's broad back draped in the overcoat.

For the first time in her life, Jeanne experienced real terror. Her mind fluttered like a trapped bird. Why hadn't she left before, when she had her chance? Retreating, she threw herself into the stuffed armchair and gathered her long legs in her arms in an attitude of submission. She listened to the sound of his approaching footsteps and turned so she wouldn't be facing him when he entered. She was prepared to show surprise, but he entered the room with barely a glance in her direction. Hands deep in his overcoat pockets, he strolled about appraising the furniture with an expression of mild disapproval.

He approached Jeanne's chair. She wanted to tell him about the key, that she had only come to return it, but she didn't want to be the first to speak. There was always a chance that he would make some indication that her presence was welcome.

But his first words were a directive. "The armchair has to go in front of the window."

Before she could speak, he grasped the armrests, and with impressive strength, half-lifted the chair, with her still sitting in it, and propelled it across the room to the window. He stood back and casually took off his overcoat, draping it over the back of another chair. He wore a soft gray houndstooth jacket and a turtleneck sweater that gave him an aura of youthfulness. He had shaved since the morning, and carefully brushed his hair. To Jeanne he looked almost distinguished. She hoped his grooming was a tribute to her. Her fear diminished. Defensively she said, "I came to return the key."

He ignored her remark.

"Come help me," he ordered.

His tone precluded any refusal. Jeanne stood up as if at attention, and slipped out of her coat, very much aware that she wore nothing beneath her skirt. She shook her head, and a mass of auburn curls tumbled about her shoulders. Her large breasts stood out hard against the sheer synthetic fabric of her dress. Paul's concentration was elsewhere.

"You didn't waste any time moving your stuff in." She pointed to the key she had left on the table. "I came to return it to *you*."

"What do I care?"

He picked up a chair and handed it to her, looking at her for the first time.

"Put the chairs around the table," he instructed.

Jeanne shrugged and obeyed. While it gave her a perverse pleasure to be ordered about by this strange man who respected none of the social amenities, it also annoyed her.

"I was going to throw the key away," she said, without turning, and she ran her fingers down the smooth, stiff support of the chair back. It was grooved and circular at the top. With her index finger she slowly circled the grain of the wood, studying her own long, slender fingernail.

"But I couldn't throw it away," she went on. "What an idiot I am."

It was a small confession, and one she was certain he would respond to. She was indicating her own apparent helplessness, and he would surely sympathize. After all, he too was human, even though there was an aura of potential violence about him.

Jeanne turned to confront him, and found that she was alone in the room.

"Listen, mister," she called irritably, her disappointment matched only by her incredulousness: he really didn't care, and that was difficult for her to understand, after what had happened before. "Where are you? I have to go."

There was no answer. For a moment she thought that he had gone, but his overcoat was still there. The fear she had experienced that morning returned.

She walked through the living room, searching for him, past the furniture shrouded in the sheet, and out into the corridor.

He stood at the entrance to the small room, staring down at the protruding mattress, one hand resting on his hip, the other braced against the wall.

"The bed is too big for the room," he said, as if that wasn't obvious.

"I don't know what to call you," Jeanne said.

"I don't have a name."

It was an odd thing to say, Jeanne thought.

"You want to know mine?" she asked.

"No."

"It's . . ."

She didn't even see the blow coming. He seemed merely to flip his wrist, but the force of the back of his hand striking her snapped her head to the side. Jeanne's mouth fell open, and her eyes were wide with surprise, anger, and terror.

"I don't want to know your name," he said menacingly, staring straight at her. "You don't have a name, and I don't have a name, either. No names here. Not one name!"

"You're crazy," Jeanne whimpered, holding her hand to her cheek. She began to cry.

"Maybe I am. But I don't want to know anything about you. I don't want to know where you live, or where you come from. I want to know nothing. Nothing! You understand?" He was practically shouting.

"You scared me," she said, wiping the tears from her cheeks.

"Nothing," he repeated. He spoke softly now, and his eyes were fixed on hers. "You and I are going to meet here, without knowing anything that goes on outside." His voice was hypnotic.

"But why?" she asked meekly.

Paul felt no pity for her. He approached and placed one hand on her throat. The skin was soft and smooth, the muscles tight beneath.

"Because," he said, "we don't need names here. We're going to forget everything that we knew—all the people, all that we do, wherever we live. We're going to forget everything."

She tried to imagine that.

"But I can't. Can you?"

"I don't know," he admitted. "Are you scared?"

She didn't answer. Slowly Paul began to work the buttons of her dress undone. He moved to kiss her, but Jeanne drew back.

"No more now," she said, her eyes lowered. "Let me go."

Paul gripped her arm. She was limp.

"Tomorrow," she murmured. She raised and kissed his hand. "Please, I'll want you more tomorrow."

They stood staring into each other's eyes—the captor and the delicate prey—both uncertain of what would happen next.

"All right," he said finally. "That's good. That way it won't become a habit."

He bent his face toward hers, catching her hair in his hand, smelling her fragrance.

"Don't kiss me," she said. "If you kiss me, I won't be able to leave."

"I'll walk you to the door."

They moved down the corridor leisurely, as if reluctant to actually part. They were not touching now, but both were keenly aware of the other's body, of the closeness and the intriguing possibility. That was the bond between them. Paul opened the door for her, and Jeanne stepped out onto the landing.

She turned to say good-bye, but the heavy door had already closed.

# Chapter
# Five

PAUL FELT no elation after Jeanne left, only a bleak dominance. He expected nothing more, and he forgot even that by the time he had returned to his hotel, smelling the reality of rotten fish where a trash can had tumbled into the gutter of his street, and hearing screams that at first he thought were caused by pain, until he realized they came from an unattended baby. He wondered if Rosa had made any outcry in her final act, and decided that she must have deserted him in silence, much the same way she had lived with him. That and the fact that she left him no explanation were further twists of the knife of discontent lodged in Paul's guts. Life in general was sordid and dirty, and a trial: every harsh sound and minor irritation grated upon him, and sometimes he could barely restrain his savage impulse.

The foyer of the *pension* was deserted. Behind the small desk, which supported only the battered register—which Paul kept only because it was required by law, and not because he cared to know the names of any of his guests—the door to his room stood open. Someone was moving about there, and he carefully slipped out of his overcoat, dropped it on the desk, and slipped through the door. He would have welcomed some struggle, but he saw that it was his mother-in-law, a stolid, middle-aged woman wearing a plain black coat and hat with a veil. Her eyes were red, and rimmed with flesh that seemed bruised. A heavy application of powder couldn't totally disguise the unhealthy pallor of her skin. She stood before an open drawer of Paul's bureau, searching among Rosa's clothes with frantic hands.

He did not disturb her. Paul had mixed emotions about Mère—that was what she asked him to call her, and it seemed easy enough—and they were not all bad. She and her sycophantic husband belonged to the petty bourgeoisie he despised, but he knew she had loved her daughter and that she had tried unsuccessfully to understand her. Paul thought he was the one who understood Rosa, and the fatuousness of that assumption as it had been so blatantly revealed to him the night before now made him more tolerant of Rosa's mother. After all, it was Mère's decision to leave them the hotel to run, but then that might have been less than a blessing. Perhaps they would have had a chance if they had left Paris. . . .

She turned and saw him. For several seconds they hesitated; then they stepped quickly toward each other and embraced. She felt very solid to Paul, and he remembered the trips he and Rosa used to take by train on Sundays, out to their cottage near Versailles. Mère always served ragoût or some other uninspired staple, and a local white wine that was dry and slighly effervescent and left no after-effects.

"I took the five-o'clock train," she said. She looked up at him with tired, grieved eyes. "Oh, God, Paul," she cried.

He could think of nothing to say to her, and dreaded her questions. Maybe she would realize the futility of questions. She turned and began to search compulsively among the scraps of paper, buttons, pins, and other personal articles on the table next to Paul's bed.

"Papa's in bed with asthma," she said. Neither she nor Paul was sorry that he hadn't come, since he had never approved either of Paul or of Rosa, but lacked the courage to complain. "The doctor wouldn't let him come. It's better like that. I'm stronger."

She moved across to the wardrobe closet and opened it without asking his permission. She searched among Rosa's dresses and ran her hand along the top shelf. One by one she took down

Rosa's handbags and piled them on the bed. She turned each one upside down, but discovered nothing except an old lipstick.

"What are you looking for?" Paul asked, his annoyance growing. Their mutual warmth might be short-lived, he suspected.

"Something that would explain it," Mère said. "A letter, a sign. It's not possible that my Rosa would leave nothing for her mother. Not even a word."

She began to weep, with long, choking sobs. Paul gathered up the handbags and replaced them, and he shut the closet door. On top of the wardrobe rested the suitcase that had contained Rosa's mementos, and he stared at it. There was no reason why she should see those things, since they explained nothing.

"I told you over the phone," he said. "She didn't leave anything. It's useless to keep looking."

He picked up her suitcase, a large canvas valise that seemed too heavy for just a brief stay. He did not want her staying long in the hotel, for the sight of her reminded him of Rosa, and of all the problems left unsolved.

"You need to rest," he told her, in a tone not to be contradicted. "There are some rooms free upstairs."

Paul led her toward the stairs. Mère noticed how worn the carpet was, and how it was pulling away from the runners at the back of each step, that the bulb of the brass lamp next to the desk was cracked, and that the clear borders of the frosted panes in the front door had not been washed in a year. The hotel also contained an odor she did not remember —like the smell of old Camembert—and she was doubly glad that her husband hadn't come with her.

They passed a black couple on the stairs. It was the Algerian who played the saxophone and his wife, both wearing coats that were slightly too large, and both smiling with displays of white, healthy teeth. Paul nodded to them, but Mère paused on the step and watched them descend. No black people had ever been allowed in the place when she managed the hotel, and she looked up at Paul in amazement. He regarded her coolly, devoid of expression. He was not going to make it easy for her to complain, and he turned before she could speak, and continued the climb.

The doors all seemed in need of painting, and this made them seem more anonymous. From one came the sound of the maid running the vacuum cleaner. Paul pushed open the next one and ushered Mère inside. A milk-glass pitcher sat on the tiny bureau, but there were no flowers. He set her valise in the middle of the bed, which sagged with the sigh of tired springs.

"With a razor?" Mère asked, and Paul winced. He knew the question would come, and yet he hadn't been prepared. To answer it was almost the equivalent of giving way to sickness.

"Yes," he said, without passion.

"What time did it happen?"

Paul would explain once, he decided, and after

that he would never speak of it again, no matter what.

"I don't know," he began. "I was on the night shift. The last guest came back about one. I closed up, and . . ."

He closed his eyes, saw the scene again—a small room washed in more blood than he would have thought possible. Rosa slumped in the tub, forbidding and austere even in that gory death. He had not been able to advance past the bed, not because he couldn't stand the sight, but because he was afraid of the razor and what he might do with it. She might have prepared him—a gesture, a word beforehand, something to soften it, or make it comprehensible. She could have arranged for the maid or the concierge, Raymond, to discover that horror. Did she want him to suffer more, or didn't she care? Either way, it was devastating.

"She killed herself during the evening," he said, ending it.

"And then?"

Her voice was like an echo; no matter what he said, Paul knew there would be another question.

"I already told you," he said, suddenly very weary. "When I found her, I called an ambulance."

He walked back out into the hall before she could speak. The room they were speaking of was directly across the hall, and Paul thought he heard water running in the tub. He pressed his ear against the rough wood. Mère had begun to unpack her bag, and didn't realize that he was gone.

"After your phone call," she said, "we stayed up all night, talking about Rosa and you."

Paul wondered if the maid had left the water running. She could have done it out of spite, or because she was afraid the blood would remain in the pipe. She was very superstitious, and Paul wondered if she was still in that room.

He returned to Mère's room. She was carefully laying out her belongings—toilet articles, a warm nightgown, a black dress for the funeral. She looked at this approvingly.

"Papa kept whispering," she went on, "as if the whole thing had happened in our house."

She looked up at him with a curious expression that he thought grotesque.

"Where did it happen?" she asked.

"In one of the rooms." Paul spoke with some contempt, pronouncing the word *chambre* as if the room was some grand salon. "What difference does it make?"

"Does anyone know if she suffered?"

How could she not have suffered? Paul thought. And why did she do it?

"You'll have to ask the doctors." He added with malicious pleasure, "They're doing an autopsy."

Her mouth opened in surprise. Autopsies were associated with crime and disrepute, and she would not allow it.

"No autopsy," she said, pretending that she was in authority.

Paul could stand no more questions. He turned

away and crossed the hall to the other door. He tried the handle, then abruptly swung the door open. The room was empty, and as tidy as it was earlier. Water gushed from the faucet into the tub, and he crossed the room and shut it off. He stared down at the clean enamel. Perhaps he should bring Mère over and show her the setting of her daughter's suicide. Perhaps that would satisfy her. Paul twisted the faucet tighter, but stopped before he broke it. The room was so common; perhaps that was why Rosa chose it.

Across the hall, Mère began to unpack bundles of cards and envelopes. They were all lined in black, appropriate only for the announcement of death. They were left over from the funerals of other relatives, and she prided herself on the knowledge and experience she had with such matters. She would handle her daughter's last rites with efficiency: Rosa would lack nothing. Paul worried her slightly. She had always been afraid of him, and at the same time recognized his intense maleness. He was so different from her own husband. Once she thought that Paul was the only kind of man who could manage Rosa, and for that reason she gave her blessing to Rosa's marriage to a soldier of fortune. It was her husband's phrase.

Paul stood in the doorway, looking down at the collection of cards and envelopes. Mère picked one up and examined it almost lovingly.

"I had them in the house," she said, avoiding his eyes. "I've been through death before. By now I think of everything. I'm going to make the room beautiful, with flowers everywhere."

Paul clenched his fists. He couldn't take much more.

"Cards and relatives," he said bitterly, "flowers and funeral clothes—all in that suitcase. You haven't forgotten a thing, except one. I don't want any priests."

That hadn't occurred to her, and a funeral without a priest was unthinkable.

"Religious," she stammered. "It's going to be a religious funeral."

"Rosa wasn't a believer!"

His words resounded down the hall. Other doors opened, as the guests began to listen. Rosa's suicide had left a pall over the entire hotel, and many of the guests moved furtively through the halls, afraid either of death or of inconvenience.

"Nobody around here is a believer," he called, for the benefit of the others.

"Don't shout, Paul," Mère said, moving fearfully backward until the bed was between them.

Paul roared, "The Church doesn't want suicides!"

It was absurd, and yet he felt agony and frustration. For a moment he thought he could have throttled her, but he turned on the door instead, and slammed it with first one and then the other massive fist, driving it hard against the wall. It trembled on the hinges, and a hush fell over the hotel.

"They'll absolve her," Mère said, crying again in desperation. "I'll see to it. We'll have a beautiful Mass. . . ." Then she sat on the bed, covered her face with her hands. "Do you know what Papa said?" she sobbed, unable to hold back what she thought was the truth. "He said, 'My little girl was always happy. What did they do to her? Why did she kill herself?' "

Paul wished that he too could cry, could do something to ease the pain. But there was nothing he could do.

"I don't know," he said. "I'll never know."

Controlling his anger, he turned and stepped quickly out into the hall. Most of the doors closed quickly, as the guests tried to hide the fact that they were listening, and a few doors remained slightly open. Paul thought of the people behind them as worms, and he wanted to provoke them, though he knew they all lacked the courage to challenge him. Their lives were as pointless as his own, and as contemptible.

With false composure he walked down the corridor, grasped the handle of every open door, and slammed it shut.

# Chapter
## Six

IN PARIS there are winter days when the breeze seems to carry all the way up from the Côte d'Azur, the sycamore trees look a little less bare against a blemishless sky, and a weak sun manages to coax the smell of life from a cold earth. It is too early even for a false spring, yet a promise hangs in the air. The color for which the city is famous stretches overhead—a Paris blue—augmented by the reds and yellows of the café awnings, the textured gray stone, and the dun-colored expanse of the Seine.

Although Paul had slept badly, sitting up in an armchair most of the night, the unusually balmy air revived him. Jeanne had resolved before falling into a dreamless sleep that she would never see him again, but that resolution weakened when she confronted the bright new day, and died even before she drank her morning coffee. The two of them arrived at the apartment on the Rue Jules Verne almost simultaneously. They stripped in the small room, and fell onto the mattress locked in an embrace. The promise of the previous day had been fulfilled. Their abstinence increased their excitement. She clutched him with her arms and legs, as if seeking some protection from their heightened passion.

For a long time afterward they lay side-by-side, without touching, waiting for some sound to penetrate the walls washed golden red in the morning sunlight. None did. The apartment contained them like a womb.

Jeanne's hair spread out like a sunburst on the ticking of the mattress, wild and abundant. Her breasts, even in repose, were firm, combining the fullness of a mature, sensual woman and the resiliency of an adolescent. Her nipples were large and dark, her skin clear and almost radiant. Her hips were as narrow as a boy's, and complemented her ample female sensuality.

Paul's body seemed merely vast in comparison with hers, and lacking in definition. He sprawled beside her like an indulgent god. His arms and chest were still powerful, and covered with hair untouched by grayness, but he was beginning to lose his muscle tone; his body did not match the austerity of his face, with its aquiline planes and lingering, fierce vitality. He seemed caught in an abrupt transition between youth and old age.

Paul was aware of Jeanne's body only in the most superficial way, since he thought of her as little more than that body, which housed his random passion, paid compliments to his vanity and his sexual acumen, and isolated him momentarily from his despair. Her voluptuousness he would have noticed only if the manifestations of it were missing. Jeanne also took his body for granted, but in an entirely different way. His initial assault upon her had been based upon a general, overwhelming masculine power, and it was in terms of force that she still saw and felt him. She didn't really see his body, though his presence was massive. The love she began to feel for him was based upon this power, and reinforced by his insistence upon secrecy—and therefore mystery.

Jeanne raised herself to her knees and pulled on her underpants.

"I like sex," she said, "because it's healthy exercise. It keeps your body in shape, and it gives you a great appetite."

She walked out of the room without looking down at him, and went into the bathroom. In the mirror she saw a tousle-headed girl with high, wide cheekbones and lips raised in a perpetual pout, and breasts that sometimes felt almost cumbersome. Her face reflected an incongruous mixture of shallowness and wisdom. Jeanne felt a sudden chill. Though the glass above the tub flooded the room with light, the turquoise-and-white tiles reflected only the crisp reality of winter. The day had grown cold. Her body seemed exposed, and devoid of all warmth, and she slammed the door behind her as if that were some protection.

Paul gathered up his clothes. He padded down the corridor on his bare feet, bound for the bathroom. The idea of washing themselves and dressing in each other's presence appealed to him, since he was determined to respect no conventions. The closed door made him pause. He considered walking directly in on her—Jeanne was at that point precariously balanced on the twin sinks, washing herself, her thighs gripping the cold stone because there was no bidet—but he preferred to be invited.

He rattled the doorknob.

"Leave me alone," she called.

"Let me watch."

"It's not very interesting."

"That depends." Her bourgeois inhibitions amused him, and he called out, "You're washing yourself. I want to see."

"No!" she said emphatically. It was so strange that she would surrender all pretensions of modesty in the act of sex, and assume them in the mundane aftermath.

She slipped gracefully from the edge of the sink and shut off the water.

"I'm finished," she said, as if he couldn't hear. "You can come in now."

Paul entered, ceremoniously cradling his clothes

in one arm. He deposited them on the edge of the tub and stepped naked to the sink, standing next to Jeanne. Her toilet articles were spread before her—mascara, lipstick, a small frosted bottle of cleansing cream—and she began to make up her face, pouting her lips, gazing sideways at her lashes, oblivious of Paul.

Paul was chuckling—a sound new to her—his hands resting on the edge of the sink.

"What's so funny?" she demanded.

"Nothing, really," he said, but he continued to laugh. "I was just picturing you perched on top of this sink. It takes practice to keep your balance and wash yourself at the same time. If you fall, you could break a leg."

Jeanne was furious, not because he was amused, but because he showed it. There were some things one didn't talk about. Color rose to her cheeks, and she turned angrily back to the mirror.

Paul decided to humor her. He kissed her lightly on the shoulder, said, "Now, don't be like that."

"We're different," she said, without looking at him.

She glanced at him in the mirror, and saw that he was still mocking her. Her reservations seemed so petty to him. They were, after all, just two bodies colliding in the abyss of the contemporary world, where one act was no more outrageous than another. Only the palpable heat of her flesh seemed real to him.

But he would still pamper her, for a time. "Forgive me," he entreated, and he kissed her again. "Do you forgive me?"

Jeanne relented. "Yes," she said, and she smiled at him, conveying a child's spontaneous warmth.

Paul recognized the proper moment to move forward again, to push her farther.

"Then come here and wash me," he said.

Her smile dissolved. "Are you kidding?" she asked in broken English. "Not on your life! What makes you think you can order me around like that?"

There was an edge to her voice—both anger and fear—but Paul ignored it. He turned on the water and began to soap his hands, and then his penis. He straddled the basin.

"You don't know what you're missing," he said.

Jeanne shook her head in disbelief. "You know what you are?" she said. "You're a pig."

"A pig?" Paul considered that: the idea was amusing.

"A toilet is a toilet," she explained with mock condescension, "and love is love. You mix up the sacred and the profane."

For Paul there was no difference between the two words, and he determined to make her see that. But for the moment he was silent. Jeanne continued to apply her makeup.

Paul dried himself, conscious of a growing malaise. The scene smacked of domesticity: they dressed in respectful silence, preparing themselves for the outside world, like a man and wife already too familiar with each other's habits. Paul decided to change that.

"I once saw a very sad Swedish film that mixed up the sacred and the profane," he began, sitting on the edge of the tub to put on his socks.

"All pornographic films are sad," she said. "They're death."

"It wasn't pornography—it was just Swedish. It was called *Secret Stockholm*—the story of a very shy young guy who finally got up the courage to invite a girl to his house. So while he's waiting, all excited, all emotional, he begins to wonder if his feet are dirty. He checks. They're disgusting. So he runs into the bathroom to wash them. But there's no water. He's desperate, he doesn't know what to do. Suddenly he gets an inspiration. He puts his foot into the toilet, and flushes. The guy's face lights up—he's done it. But when he tries to take his foot out of the toilet, he can't. It's stuck. He tries again, he pulls it every which way, but no luck. The girl comes and finds him desperate, crying, leaning against the wall, with his foot in the toilet bowl."

Paul seemed to take pleasure in the sadistic aspects of his story.

He continued, "The guy tells the girl to go away, and never to come back. But she insists that she can't leave him like that, because he'll starve to death. She goes to get a plumber. The plumber studies the case, but doesn't want to take the responsibility. 'I can't break the toilet,' he says. 'It might hurt his foot.' They call an ambulance. The attendants arrive with a stretcher, and they all decide to unbolt the toilet from the floor. The boy is put on the stretcher, with the toilet still on his foot, like an enormous shoe. The two attendants begin to giggle. The first one slips down the stairs, falls under the stretcher. The toilet falls on his head and kills him instantly."

Jeanne laughed nervously. Paul stood up abruptly and walked out of the bathroom, leaving her alone. The cruel humor was something they could at least have shared, but he was unwilling.

Fully dressed now, Paul began to pace the circular living room, inspecting it with a clinical eye. He moved the table and chairs into the dining room, and dragged the heavy double mattress in from the small room. What had been a tabernacle isolating them from the outside world took on the aspects of an arena. He raised the shutters on one of the windows slightly, to allow more light to enter the room.

Jeanne emerged from the bathroom, perfectly made-up and ready to leave. Her hair was brushed and shining, and carefully rolled and pinned high above the back of her neck. They looked at each other. Jeanne smiled, hesitated, gave a little wave, and turned toward the front door. But Paul wasn't through with her yet, and somehow she knew it: there was no need for him to call her back.

She returned to the living room. Paul stood in the sunlight, his chin raised, regarding her with the same cool detachment. She returned his gaze. They were now two combatants, taking each other's measure.

"Shall we begin again?" she asked.

Paul didn't answer, but slowly began to unbutton his shirt. Jeanne tossed her coat and bag aside, and imitated him, stripping away her blouse and pants, finally standing naked and proud before him.

"We want to look at each other," she said. "Is that it?"

"Yes," he said, and for the first time he looked at her as a woman. "That's it."

They sat on the bed, facing each other, and entwined their legs. He felt her face with both hands, as if he had just discovered it, her neck and shoulders, her breasts—where he lingered, marveling at their fullness.

"Isn't it beautiful like this?" he said, believing it, "without knowing anything?"

"Adam and Eve didn't know anything about each other," she said.

"We're like them in reverse. They saw they were naked, and were ashamed. We saw that we had clothes on, and we came here to be naked."

They entwined their legs in a seated position of the Kama Sutra, each of them with one thigh resting over the other's. Jeanne took his penis in her hand and guided him into her. Paul ran his fingers over her hips and stroked the warm mound of her pubic hair.

"I think we could come without touching," she said.

They leaned back on their arms and regarded each other.

"With our eyes," she said, "and bodies."

He asked jokingly, "Did you come yet?"

"No."

Paul rocked back and forth.

Jeanne moaned, "It's difficult."

"I didn't either, yet. You're not trying hard enough."

Their movements quickened. Paul reached his climax first, and slipped away from her. But Jeanne had never been more content. For the first time they began to feel something besides lust and the excitement of an illicit affair; it was a kind of liking. She wanted to call him something, but didn't know what.

"I know what I'll do," she said brightly. "I shall have to invent a name for you."

"A name? Oh, Jesus Christ!" Paul said, laughing and shaking his head. "Oh, God, I've been called by a million names in my life. I don't want a name. I'm better off with a grunt or a groan. Do you want to know my name?"

He raised himself on his hands and knees. He formed his mouth into the shape of a snout, lifted his head, and growled loudly. Then he began to grunt, deep in his throat—a primal sound that excited them both. Jeanne put her arms around his neck and moved one foot up between his legs.

"It's so masculine," she said. "Now, listen to mine."

She pulled him down next to her on the mattress and held him tightly. She trilled, then asked, "Do you like it?"

They laughed. He grunted again, and she answered. Together they filled the circular room with the strident courtship of beasts.

# Chapter
## Seven

TOM'S CREW was waiting in the garden of the villa in suburban Chatillon-sous-Bagneux when Jeanne arrived. Her hair was no longer up in a roll, but clustered in wild curls about her shoulders. She looked as if she had just awakened. Fresh from her tryst with Paul, she brimmed with life; in contrast, the others looked like statues, and she paused by the gate to watch the soundman. He knelt by his Nagra, earphones clamped in place, and passed the shotgun mike back and forth above his head, recording the varied strident sounds of barnyard animals. The cameraman loaded film into the Arriflex, both hands thrust into a black bag. The script girl thumbed through the glossy pages of *Elle*, obviously bored. None of them were interested in the geese that waddled by: the birds simply produced an interesting sound.

Jeanne slammed the gate.

"Thanks for the noise," the soundman said. "That was discretion itself."

Jeanne saw the disappointment on Tom's face. He stood off to one side, his hands in his pockets, trying to smile at her.

"You're not ready," he said, gazing at her hair.

She decided she wouldn't excuse herself by lying. "But it's not a wig," she joked. "It's mine. Am I not beautiful? Tell me you don't like the way I look."

"But I do like the way you look," Tom insisted. "You seem changed, but you're the same. I can already see a shot . . ."

Tom raised both hands, and, in imitation of a camera, circled her. The crew prepared for the shot. Jeanne looked around at the garden and the encompassing stone wall. In her childhood, the villa had been surrounded on three sides by green fields, and it seemed inviolate, like all her memories. It was with disappointment that she had watched those same fields over the years become choked with concrete apartment buildings and the shantytowns of impoverished immigrants forced out of the cities.

"The camera is high," Tom went on. "It slowly descends toward you. And as you advance, it moves in on you. There's music, too. It gets closer and closer to you. . . ."

"I'm in a hurry," Jeanne interrupted. "Let's begin."

"But first we'll talk about it a little."

"No," she said.

The crew scrambled into action, and followed her toward the back of the garden.

"Today we improvise," she announced. "You will just have to keep up."

Tom was delighted. He motioned for his cameraman to follow. "You're lovely," he said, walking behind her, reaching just to touch her wild hair. "It's the natural you, at home in your childhood setting. It couldn't be any other way! I'll film you as you were—wild, impetuous, ravishing!"

Jeanne led them to a small grave next to the hawthorn bush. The photograph set in the tombstone showed her German shepherd sitting obediently. Engraved beneath it were the words "Mustapha: Oran 1950–Paris 1958."

"He was my childhood friend," she said. "He used to watch me for hours, and I thought he understood me."

An old woman wearing a black dress, her arms crossed on her heavy bosom, came hurrying toward them from the house. Her white hair was pulled severely back, and she reached the group in time to hear what Jeanne said. The woman added, "Dogs are worth more than people. Much more."

Jeanne jumped up and hugged her. "This is Olympia," she explained to Tom. "My childhood nurse."

"Mustapha could always tell the rich from the poor," Olympia said. "He never made a mistake.

If someone who was well dressed came in, he never moved. . . ."

Her husky voice trailed off as she watched the cameraman, encouraged by Tom, begin to circle her.

"If a beggar showed up," she went on, "you should have seen him. What a dog! The Colonel trained him to recognize Arabs by their odor."

Jeanne turned to the crew. "Olympia is an anthology of domestic virtues. She is faithful, admiring . . . and racist."

The old woman led them into the villa.

Potted plants crowded the entrance hall, haphazardly distributed over the worn tiles. A faded rattan side table supported a brass lamp with a chimney of bottle-green glass; above it hung an amateur oil painting of Jeanne's father, the Colonel, in full dress. His uniform was exquisitely cut, his boots unmarked, his moustache full and waxed.

Jeanne led the crew past the picture, into an adjoining room with bare polished floors and walls hung with cloth printed in bold geometric designs. Primitive weapons neatly arranged above a shelf of photographs, the glut of exotic scenes yellowing and curling at the edges, momentarily distracted the crew and their director.

Jeanne watched them proudly. She took a frame from the shelf and held it up for their inspection: in the photograph, three rows of elementary-school girls confronted the camera dourly, under the eye of a stalwart woman in walking shoes.

"That's me," said Jeanne. "To the right of the teacher, Mademoiselle Sauvage. She was very religious, very severe—"

"She was too good," interrupted Olympia. "She spoiled you."

Tom slapped the cameraman on the shoulder; he swiveled, pointed the lens toward the old woman, but she ducked behind the others.

Jeanne pointed at another figure.

"And that's Christine, my best friend. She married a pharmacist and has two children. It's a little like a village here. Everybody knows everybody. . . ."

Olympia croaked, "Personally, I couldn't live in Paris. It's more human here."

Again the cameraman pivoted, in search of a new quarry; Olympia retreated through the louvered doors.

"We're sheltered here," Jeanne went on. "It's melancholy to look behind you."

They moved into her childhood room. Stuffed animals worn bare at the edges were marshaled along the windowsills, scarred wooden replicas of adult possessions—a wheelbarrow, a chair, a footstool—lined the walls. The book covers were all faded.

"Why is it melancholy?" Tom asked her. "It's marvelous."

She simply raised her hands and turned around.

"It's you!" he cried. "It's your childhood—everything I want!"

Tom gazed at the ceiling in inspiration. At the same time, he motioned for the cameraman to follow Jeanne.

"These notebooks are the childhood of your intelligence. It's fascinating. The public is a little afraid of the woman of today. . . ."

He paused to think, forming the script in his mind, while Jeanne danced out of the room, the cameraman in pursuit.

". . . But if you can show the daily intelligence of some woman or other, slightly above average, but not unattainable . . ."

Inspired, Tom gazed around, and seemed to notice the crew members for the first time, lurking behind them.

"What are you doing there?" he shouted. "Who are all these zombies around us?"

He chased them outside, then opened a door leading into a room filled with low, comfortable furniture.

"I'm opening the door!" he cried, beckoning to Jeanne. "I'm opening all of the doors!"

"Where are you going?" she asked, trying to match his enthusiasm.

"I have a plan. Reverse gear! Understand? Like a car put in reverse."

He took her by the hands.

"Close your eyes," he said. "Back up, keep going, find your childhood again."

"I see Papa," she said, cooperating, "in full dress uniform . . ."

"Don't be afraid. Overcome the obstacles."

"Papa in Algiers . . ."

"You are fifteen," he said. "Fourteen, thirteen, twelve, eleven, ten, nine . . ."

"I see my favorite street when I was eight . . ."

She opened her eyes and picked up a bound ledger lying on the table. She began to read aloud.

" 'Homework for French class. Theme: the country. Development: the country is a land of cows. The cow is entirely covered with leather. It has four sides—the front, the back, the top, and the bottom. . . .' "

"Charming!"

Jeanne picked up the dictionary and began to leaf through it.

"The source of my culture was the Larousse," she said. "I copied from it."

She read in a loud, theatrical voice: "Menstruation, feminine noun, physiological function consisting of flow. . . . Penis, masculine noun, organ of copulation measuring from five to forty centimeters. . . ."

"Very instructive," he said, turning toward the window and signaling for the crew to return.

Jeanne took down a photograph of her father. She studied the array of medals on his chest, the gold braid of his dress uniform that she remembered so vividly, the way he stood at attention with his fingers slightly curled at his sides. She had never seen him when he wasn't formal. He was always kind, and yet she had never felt completely free just to climb into his lap, to kiss and touch him. Her mother worshiped the Colonel, and Jeanne had often detected what even then seemed to her to be jealousy on her mother's part. Jeanne had even wanted to be a soldier like the Colonel, to carry a weapon and move through life with his splendid assurance. She was so flattered when he offered to teach her to shoot his service pistol that she overcame her terror of the gun's roar and the potential death it dispensed, and learned to shoot almost as well as he. Jeanne thought of the Colonel as an old man, but an invincible one, and when he died it was as if the whole world was left in danger.

"Who is this?" asked Tom, holding up a pencil drawing of a young boy playing a piano.

Jeanne smiled. "My first love," she said. "My cousin Paul."

The cameraman moved between them, focusing the Arriflex on the picture. Olympia stood in the doorway, massively silent.

"Why are his eyes closed?" the script girl asked.

"He was playing the piano, and he played magnificently. I remember him seated there, running his slender fingers over the keys. He practiced for hours."

She did remember her cousin's dark eyes and unhealthy, feverish stare. While his parents and hers drank tea in the sitting room, looking out at the blooming hyacinth and the hawthorn, talking of their travels in Africa, she and he slipped quietly away. . . .

Jeanne opened the window and pointed toward the backyard. "Those two trees," she said, "the chestnut and the plane tree, were where we used to sit. We each had our own tree, and we'd look at each other. My cousin seemed like a saint to me."

She took Tom's hand and led him out into the yard. "Aren't they beautiful?" she said, and she pointed to a lot overgrown with weeds and bushes. But Jeanne didn't see this, for she was locked into a reverie of what had been, and she was looking up instead of at the decline all around her. "Aren't they beautiful?" she said again, as if Tom couldn't see for himself. "To me, those trees seemed like a real jungle."

How easy it was to idealize for Tom. His enthusiasm and his disappointments encouraged her to indulge her own penchant for fantasy. But she couldn't go on. Reality was massing about her like storm clouds, and the more sordid aspects of her childhood threatened to be revealed.

Olympia came lumbering after them, holding up the photograph of her father like an icon. "The Colonel was superb!" she called to anyone who would listen, trying to get the cameraman to focus on what she considered the most important facet of the villa. "He even frightened me," she admitted.

Jeanne looked at the photograph again, and remembered the fear she had often felt when he was displeased. Suddenly she was thinking of Paul, of his conceit and his strength, and she wanted to cling to him. She looked around her, and saw for the first time the way the villa walls lacked paint, the erosion of one corner of the garden, the crumbling stone and weeds and the view of tarpaper shacks in the distance.

"None of that existed in my time," she said with disgust, pushing her way into the thicket, the crew close behind her. She felt chastened and somehow cheated by her visit, and when she saw half a dozen little dark-skinned boys squatting among the blackberry bushes, defecating, she became angry—as if she were being violated.

"What are you doing?" she shouted at them as they pulled up their pants and fled.

Jeanne grabbed one of the boys by the arm and shook him. His clothes were little more than rags, and he trembled as he kicked at her shins. Jeanne saw Olympia pick up a broken board and come charging through the thicket, the cameraman galloping beside her and keeping her in focus.

"Don't you have anyplace besides my jungle to do this in?" Jeanne asked the boy, and realized that he couldn't understand her.

"Run fast," she said. "Beat it!"

He was gone, scrambling over the wall like an animal.

"If I catch you, I'll hang you!" screamed Olympia. "Go shit in your own country, you little bastard."

Olympia picked up a stone and hurled it futilely after the trespassers. "Africa," she said disgustedly. "You can't even live at home anymore."

Jeanne turned and looked at the scene around her, and she said to herself, "Growing old is a crime."

Tom caught up with her, breathing heavily, and he gestured toward the cameraman. His face was flushed with excitement and pride.

"Did you get it?" Jeanne asked.

"All of it."

"Olympia was magnificent. Now you'll have a precise idea of race relations in the suburbs."

Jeanne realized that her eyes were moist.

Tom didn't notice. "Now tell me about your father," he said.

"I thought we were finished for the day."

She turned away from him and started for the front gate. Tom suddenly seemed bound up in her illusions of childhood, vain and naïve.

"One last thing," he said, hurrying to keep up with her.

"I'm in a hurry."

"Only five minutes, Jeanne," and his voice sounded surprised and hurt. "What about the Colonel?"

"I have a business appointment," she told him, lying easily. She went straight out the gate and didn't bother to close it.

# Chapter
# Eight

THE PROMISE of morning faded as a cover
of clouds drew across the sun. It shone through
them briefly, like a thin wafer, then darkened.
Winter rain obscured the face of Paris, driven by
the wind, and disintegrated against the tall, curved
panes of the apartment windows. Pale refracted
light played over the living-room walls, creating
the illusion of running water. By the afternoon the
room had begun to smell of sex.

They lay naked on the mattress, Jeanne's arm
resting across Paul's broad chest, her face turned
away from him. Paul held a bright silver harmonica
in his hand, and he blew into it, producing only
plaintive, disconnected notes.

"What a life," she said, speaking as if in a dream. "No time to rest."

The morning was still with her, and the villa's entombed memories. She felt an unreasonable desire to share her disappointment with Paul.

"The Colonel," she began, "had green eyes and shiny boots. I loved him like a god. He was so handsome in his uniform."

Without stirring, Paul said, "What a steaming pile of horse shit."

"What?" she felt outraged. "I forbid you—"

"All uniforms are bullshit, everything outside this place is bullshit. Besides, I don't want to hear your stories about your past, and all that."

She knew she was foolish to expect him to sympathize, but she went on, "He died in 1958, in Algeria."

"Or '68," Paul said. "Or '28, or '98."

"In '58! And I forbid you to joke about that!"

"Listen," he said patiently, "why don't you stop talking about things that don't matter here? So what the hell's the difference?"

"So what do I have to say?" she asked wearily, seeking guidance. "What do I have to do?"

Paul smiled at her. He played a few bars of a childish tune on the harmonica, with feeling and skill, then he sang, "Come on the good ship, Lollypop . . ."

Jeanne just shook her head. His distance seemed vast.

"Why don't you go back to America?" she asked.

"I don't know. Bad memories, I guess."

"Of what?"

"My father," he said, rolling onto his stomach and raising himself on his elbows, so that his face was close to hers. "He was a drunk, tough"—he stressed the word—"a whore-fucker, bar fighter, super masculine. Yeah, he was tough."

His face softened. "My mother was very poetic, also a drunk, and my memories when I was a kid were of her being arrested in the nude. We lived in a small town, in a farming community. I'd come home from school and she'd be gone—in jail or something."

A barely perceptible expression of pleasure passed over his face, softening his features. It had been so long since he had thought of these things, that they had ceased to exist for him.

"I used to have to milk a cow," he said, "every morning and every night, and I liked that. But I remember one time I was all dressed up to go out and take this girl to a basketball game, and my father said, 'You have to milk the cow.' And I asked him, 'Would you please milk it for me?' Know what he said? He said, 'Get your ass out there!' So I went out, and I was in a hurry, and I didn't have time to change my shoes, and I got cow shit all over them. On the way to the basketball game, it smelled in the car."

Paul grimaced.

"I don't know," he said, trying to dismiss what he had already recalled. "I can't remember very many good things."

Jeanne persisted. "Not one?" she asked, in English, flattering him. The memories fascinated her.

"Some," he said, relenting. "There was a farmer, a very nice old guy who worked real hard. I used to work in a ditch with him, draining land for farming. He wore overalls and he smoked a clay pipe, and half the time he wouldn't put tobacco in it. I hated the work—it was hot and dirty, and broke my back—and all day long I'd watch the old man's spit, which would run down the pipe stem and hang on the bowl. I used to make bets with myself on when it was going to fall off, and I always lost. I never saw it fall off. I'd just look around, and it'd be gone, and then the new spit would be there."

Paul laughed soundlessly and shook his head. Jeanne was afraid to move, because he might stop talking.

"And then we had a beautiful dog," he went on, in a voice that she had not heard before. It was almost a whisper. "My mother taught me to love nature—I guess that was the most she could do—and in front of our house we had this big field. It was a mustard field in the summer, and our big black dog, named Dutchy, used to hunt for rabbits there. But she couldn't see them, so she'd have to leap up in the air in this field, and look around quickly to see where the rabbits were. It was very beautiful, but she never caught the rabbits."

Jeanne laughed aloud. Paul looked at her in surprise.

"You've been had," she said triumphantly.

"Oh, really?"

She mocked his sonorous voice, speaking English with a heavy accent, "I don't want to know anything about your past, baby." It came out *beby*.

Paul lay back and regarded her coldly. Jeanne stopped laughing.

"You think I was telling you the truth?" he asked, and when she didn't speak, he added, "Maybe, maybe not."

Nonetheless, Jeanne felt that he had somehow been rendered more human.

It was she who initiated their third sexual dalliance of the day.

She said playfully, "I'm Little Red Riding Hood, and you're a wolf."

Paul began to growl, deep in his throat, but she silenced him by placing her hand on his lips. With the other she caressed his broad biceps.

"What strong arms you have," she said.

Paul decided to play Jeanne's game, but he would play for his own ends, and with his own cruel humor. He had given up enough to her already.

He said, "The better to squeeze a fart out of you."

She examined his hand. "What long nails you have."

"The better to scratch your ass with."

She ran her hand through his pubic hair. "What a lot of fur you have."

"The better to let your crabs hide."

She peered into his mouth. "Oh, what a long tongue you have!"

"The better to"—Paul paused for effect—"stick in your rear, my dear."

Jeanne took his penis in her hand and squeezed it.

"What's this for?" she asked.

"That's your happiness," he told her, "and my hap-*penis*."

Jeanne didn't understand the joke. "Peanuts?" she said, thinking that was the word he had used.

Paul welcomed the opportunity to display his type of erudition.

"Shlong," he said, while she maintained her grip. "Wienerwurst, cazzo, dick, prick, joint . . ."

She was charmed by his unabashed pride in the male organ.

"It's funny," she said, "this is like playing grown-ups when you're little. I feel like a child again here."

"Did you have fun as a kid?" Paul asked absently. Her hand on him he accepted as both a tribute and stimulation, in that order.

"It's the most beautiful thing," she said, away from the villa now and open to the swarm of idealized memories. Paul expected this, and decided to destroy her memories—leisurely and in keeping with the mood.

"It's the most beautiful thing to be made into a tattletale," he said, breathing heavily, "or forced to admire authority or sell yourself for a piece of candy."

"I wasn't like that."

"No?"

"I was writing poems. I was drawing castles—big castles with big towers."

"You never thought about sex?"

"No sex," she said emphatically.

"No, no sex." He pretended to believe her. "You were probably in love with your teacher, then."

"My teacher was a woman."

"Then she was a lesbian."

"How did you know?" She was both angered and amazed by his instincts. She dimly remembered her teacher—Mademoiselle Sauvage—who made a point of scolding the girls so she could comfort them later. Was everything to prove corrupt? she wondered.

"It's a classic situation," Paul said. "Anyway, go on."

"My first love was my cousin Paul."

The name—any name—annoyed him. "I'm going to get a hemorrhoid if you keep telling me names. I don't mind if you tell the truth, but don't give me the names."

Jeanne apologized. She was reluctant to continue, but he understood her vulnerability, and warmed to the attack.

"Well, go on," he said. "And tell the truth."

"I was thirteen. He was dark, very thin. I can see him, and his big nose. It was romance—I fell in love with him when I heard him playing the piano."

"You mean when he first got into your knickers."

Paul eased one hand along her thigh, until the tips of his fingers touched the outer lips of her vagina. He pretended to play an imaginary keyboard with the other.

"He was a child prodigy," Jeanne said. "He was playing with both hands."

"I'll bet he was." Paul snorted contemptuously. "Probably getting his kicks."

"We were dying of the heat . . ."

"Good excuse. What else?"

"In the afternoon, when the grown-ups were napping . . ."

"You started grabbing his joint."

"You're crazy," she said, with exasperation.

"Well," Paul asserted, "he touched you."

"I never let him. Never!"

Paul sensed the conflict in her. She seemed close to some revelation, and he taunted her, chanting, "Liar, liar, pants on fire, nose as long as a telephone wire! You mean to tell me that he didn't touch you? Look me straight in the eye and say, 'He didn't touch me once.' Go on, do it."

Jeanne moved back from him, and looked down at her own body. Her breasts and thighs seemed heavy and sensual; she felt so much older, so removed from that remembered time. She wanted to stop remembering, but Paul wouldn't let her.

"No," she admitted, "he touched me. But the way he did it . . ."

Paul was standing over her now. "The way he did it," he said sarcastically. "Okay, what'd he do?"

"Behind the house there were two trees, a sycamore and a chestnut. I sat under the sycamore, and he sat under the chestnut. We'd count one, two, three, and we'd each begin to masturbate. The first one who came . . ."

She looked up and saw that Paul had turned away.

"Why aren't you listening to me?" she asked, switching back into French.

He didn't answer. He knew that even her innocence was sexual, and her confession was his triumph, but he wasn't finished yet.

They were startled by the unfamiliar clamor of the doorbell. A nasal masculine voice reached them from the landing: "The complete Bible, a unique edition, without cuts . . ."

Paul was enraged by the interruption. He moved toward the door, but Jeanne stood and grabbed his arm.

"Did we make a pact or not?" she whispered. "Nobody will ever see us together. You could kill me, and nobody would ever know. Not even that Bible salesman out there."

Paul placed his hands on her throat, and her breasts brushed his forearm.

"The true Bible!" the salesman called. "Don't close your door to eternity!"

Paul detested the man without even seeing him. "Biblical pig!" he muttered. He wanted to punish the man for disturbing them, but Jeanne wouldn't release him. He began to squeeze her neck. "You're right," he said. "No one would know. Not the Bible salesman, and not that half-blind concierge."

"You don't even have a motive." She clutched his wrists, which seemed hard as wood. "The perfect crime."

His fingers tightened. He could feel the tendons in her neck; his thumbs met little resistance. How easy it would have been to conclude her banal memories, and his ability to learn them. Flesh, once corrupted, was as good as dead—Jeanne's, Rosa's, even his own. She had gotten him to reveal some of his past, and his weakness in which his rage was rooted. Someone else should suffer, and if not the Bible salesman, then her, for there was no one else at hand.

He released her, and Jeanne knelt on the mattress, clutching her neck. She breathed heavily, and wondered if he was only trying to frighten her.

The sound of the Bible salesman's receding footsteps barely reached them.

"When did you first come?" Paul asked her. "How old were you?"

"The first time?" She tried to remember, relieved and somewhat flattered. How difficult he was to fathom, and how alone, standing outlined against the window as gray as wet slate. The muscles in his back were flexed, as if he expected some assault.

"I was very late for school," she began. "Suddenly I felt a strong sensation, here." Jeanne touched her vagina. "I came as I ran. Then I ran faster and faster, and the more I ran, the more I came. Two days later I tried running again, but no dice."

Paul did not turn around. She lay face-down on the mattress, her hand still thrust between her legs. It seemed strange to be telling him the dark secrets, which she could never share with Tom.

"Why don't you listen to me?" she asked.

Paul just walked into the adjoining room. He felt as tight as a drawn wire. He sat on the edge of a chair and watched Jeanne. She began to move her hips in a circular motion, in simulation of intercourse. Her buttocks clenched.

"You know," she sighed, without looking at him, "it seems to me I'm talking to the wall."

She continued to manipulate herself with mounting pleasure.

"Your solitude weighs on me. It isn't indulgent or generous—you're an egotist." Her voice was distant, breathless. "I can be by myself too, you know."

Paul watched her rhythmically undulating young body, and his eyes filled with tears. He didn't weep for the loss of her fanciful childhood, or his own sordid beginnings. He wept for his own isolation.

Jeanne writhed into climax, and then lay still, drained and physically exhausted.

"Amen," he said.

For a long time he sat without moving. Finally she rose, and without looking at Paul, gathered her clothes together and walked into the bathroom.

Paul's jacket hung from a clothes tree.

The salt-and-pepper houndstooth weave seemed common enough to Jeanne, and on impulse she checked the label, and found that it came from Printemps, a large department store near the Opéra. She hesitated, then delved into his pockets, drew out a few coins, a used Métro ticket from Bir Hakeim, and a broken cigarette. She moved to the breast pocket, amazed at her own audacity, and discovered a wad of one-hundred-franc notes, but no papers or identification.

The door swung open suddenly, and Paul came in. He wore his trousers, and he carried an old leather brief case in one hand. He propped it on the sink and took out his shaving cream, soap, a long leather strap worn slick from the passage of many blades, and the straight razor with the bone handle.

"What am I doing in this apartment with you?" she asked him.

Paul ignored her. He began to lather his face.

"Love?" she suggested.

"Let's just say we're taking a flying fuck at a rolling doughnut."

She didn't understand exactly what he said, but she knew it was some obscene metaphor describing his view of human endeavor.

"So you think I'm a whore."

Jeanne had difficulty pronouncing the last word in English, and Paul teased her. "I think you're a what? A *war*?"

"Whore!" she shouted. "Whore, whore."

A PORTFOLIO OF PHOTOGRAPHS
FROM BERNARDO BERTOLUCCI'S

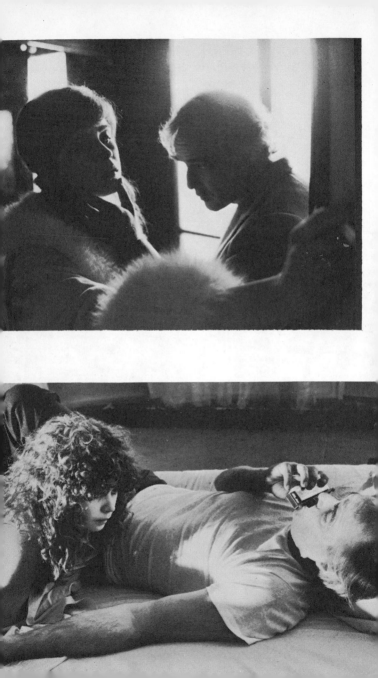

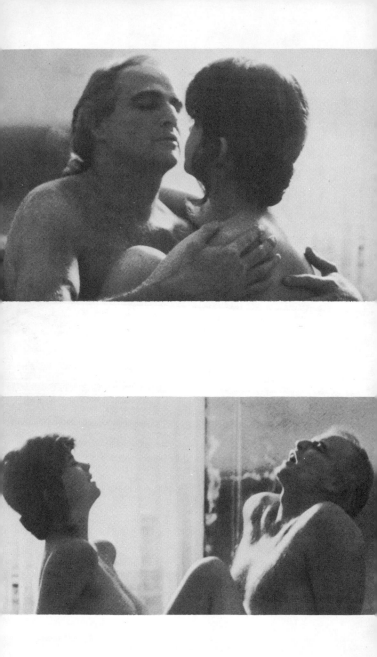

"No, you're just a dear, old-fashioned girl trying to get along."

The tone of his voice insulted her. "I prefer to be a whore."

"Why were you going through my pockets?" he said.

Jeanne managed to betray no surprise. "To find out who you are."

"To find out who you are," he repeated. "Well, if you look real close, you'll see me hiding behind my zipper."

She applied her mascara. Paul attached the razor strap to the faucet and began to whip the blade of the razor expertly over it.

"We know he buys his clothes in a big store," Jeanne said. "That's not much, folks, but that's a beginning."

"That's not a beginning, that's a finish."

The earlier mood in the circular room had passed. The cold tiles about them had a chilling effect, but Jeanne persisted. She casually asked Paul his age.

"I'll be ninety-three this weekend," he said.

"Oh? You don't look it."

He began to shave with long, precise strokes.

"Have you been to college?" she asked.

"Oh, yeah. I went to the University of the Congo. Studied whale fucking."

"Barbers don't usually go to university."

"Are you telling me that I look like a barber?"

"No," she said, "but that's a barber's razor."

"Or a madman's."

There was no humor in his voice.

"So you want to cut me up?" she decided.

"That would be like writing my name on your face."

"Like they do the slaves?"

"Slaves are branded on the ass," he said. "And I want you free."

"Free." The word sounded strange to her. "I'm not free."

She looked at his reflection in the mirror. Paul held his chin high, watching the razor's progress over the corridor of his throat. His masculinity seemed threatened in that one unguarded moment.

"Do you know what?" she said. "You don't want to know anything about me because you hate women. What have they ever done to you?"

"Either they always pretend to know who I am, or they pretend that I don't know who they are. And that's very boring."

"I'm not afraid to say who I am. I'm twenty years old . . ."

"Jesus Christ!" he said, turning on her. "Don't wear out your brain!"

Jeanne started to speak again, but he held up the razor.

"Shut up! Do you get it? I know it's tough, but you're going to have to bear it."

Jeanne relented.

Paul dropped the razor into the bag. He rinsed his face, dried it, then gripped the edges of the sink and tested its solidity.

"They're very rare," he said softly. "You don't find them anymore. I think it's the sinks that make us stay together, don't you think?"

He reached over and touched each of her toilet articles with his blunt fingers, almost delicately.

"I think I'm happy with you," he said.

He kissed her unexpectedly, gently, and then turned and left the room.

*"Encore!"* Jeanne called after him. "Do it again, again!"

She hurriedly completed her toilet, pleased with his admission. She dressed, and called to him gaily in French, "I'm coming, I'm almost ready."

She opened the door and stepped into the dim hallway.

"Can we leave together?" she asked, knowing now that he wouldn't object.

But there was no answer. Paul had already left.

# Chapter Nine

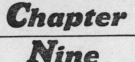

DARK blossoms formed a barricade before the window, seemed to clog the tub and sink, claimed the bureau. The bed remained empty. Paul stood in the open doorway, surveying his mother-in-law's handiwork. He was reluctant to enter. The thick, cloying odor of chrysanthemums sickened him, as did the obsequious words of his concierge, Raymond, whose manner reminded him of a mortician's.

"Looks good," Raymond said, stepping into the room ahead of Paul. "Don't you think so?"

"Only Rosa is missing."

"Your mother-in-law needed something to do. This is a nice quiet room, if only it wasn't for the closet. It's wormy—you can hear them in the wood."

Raymond pressed his bald head against the wardrobe closet and made a sound resembling that of chewing.

"I always put South Americans in this room," he said, with an evil smirk. "South Americans never leave tips. *No tengo dinero,* they always say. *Mañana, mañana.*"

Paul joked bitterly, "We're full up, mister. Only the funeral room's free."

Raymond's laugh sounded like a gasp. "That's good, boss. It does you good to laugh."

Paul turned away and descended the stairs to the foyer. A heavily made-up woman of indeterminate age, wearing a sequined skirt beneath her coat, leaned over the open registration book, searching for the names of likely customers. She was a guest, and a friend of Rosa's, and Paul tolerated her. He slammed the register closed in passing, and continued on into his own room, leaving the door open.

"No interesting new faces today," the prostitute said. "Want to bet the races, Paul?"

Paul didn't answer. He took a metal canister and a battered pot from beneath the stove and went through the motions of making coffee.

"Poor Rosa and I used to know a woman who gave us tips," she went on, not caring whether or not he listened. "Betting was a distraction. And Rosa loved horses so much. We were planning to buy one together."

"Rosa didn't know anything about horses," Paul said.

"What are you talking about? Rosa knew a lot about horses. The circus people taught her to ride."

Paul took his seat behind the desk. The woman's prattling annoyed him.

"What circus people?" he asked wearily.

"Rosa ran away when she was thirteen, and followed the circus. It's funny she never told you about it."

Paul wanted to silence her. The idea of his wife making up fabrications for a prostitute's pleasure revolted him almost as much as did the sight of this woman's opalescently white calves. Was it possible that she knew more about Rosa than he? She sensed his displeasure and went up the stairs.

"Why did she do it?" Paul heard her say. "Sunday was the Grand Prix at Auteuil."

A young man in a trench coat stood before Paul. He knew the man was an American because he carried a flight bag, he waited to be spoken to, and he had the eyes of something hunted that Paul had seen so often.

"You want a room?" Paul asked in French, out of spite.

"Yes. I'm from Düsseldorf. The winter is very long there."

It was the same phrase they all used. The tawdry theatrics of army deserters seemed pathetic to Paul. But they were paying customers, a habit rather than a necessity.

"And you left without saying anything?" Paul said.

The young man nodded. "About the passport. I'll have one in a couple of days."

Paul took a key from the board and led the way upstairs. He opened the door of the room next to Rosa's funeral parlor and watched as the young man dropped his bag on the bed and turned to him with an expression of gratitude.

"About the money," he said, "I don't know when I'll be able to pay you."

Paul just looked at him. He no longer cared about the money, but neither did he care to offer solicitude. He shut the door in the deserter's face and turned back toward the stairs.

# Chapter Ten

THE SIGHT of a pretty girl weeping on the Avenue John Kennedy should have attracted more attention. The streetlamps blinked on one by one, frail and unnecessary compared to the blaze of car lights massed almost bumper to bumper, locked in a maniacal struggle for position, loud and indifferent to the human beings who clung to the pavement. The men Jeanne passed looked first at her legs, and then her breasts, and by the time they saw her tears she was past them.

She wiped her sleeve across her eyes and turned impulsively into a restaurant. The stark white light and the greasy smell of meat cooking on skewers confronted her, and she moved quickly through the loud ranks of shopgirls and clerks toward the telephone booth in the rear.

She located a *jeton* in the bottom of her purse, deposited it, and dialed Tom's number. He answered almost immediately, and she found she couldn't speak. Annoyed by the silence, Tom began to swear.

"Just as I imagined," she said, "you get vulgar right away. . . . Listen, I have to talk to you, and I don't have time to explain. . . . I'm in Passy. . . . No, not over the telephone. . . . Meet me at the Métro stop. . . ."

She began to cry again, and hung up. Everyone wanted something from her; there was no time to rest—no quarter. They were using her up; something must be eliminated. She thought of Tom's camera probing the hidden crevices of her life. Surely that was expendable.

She left the *brasserie* and hurried back to the Métro station. She stood on the platform across the tracks from the one where Tom would arrive, her hands shoved deep in her coat pockets, watching the bright red trains come and go. She thought of Paul, and her tears dried. Her ambivalence tormented her.

Tom stood on the opposite platform, staring at her. "What are you doing over there?" he said.

"I have to talk to you."

He headed for the stairs, but Jeanne stopped him. "Don't come," she shouted. "Stay there."

Tom was as annoyed as he was confused. He

looked up and down the platform before asking her, "Why wouldn't you tell me over the telephone? Why here?"

Because only here there was enforced distance, she wanted to say. Here she was safe, at least for the moment.

"You must find someone else," she told him.

"For what?"

"For your film."

Tom seemed in agony. "Why?"

"Because you're taking advantage of me," she said. "Because you force me to do things I've never done before. Because you take up my time . . ."

They were the charges she wanted to bring against Paul, but couldn't, and the frustration and the fatigue brought fresh tears to her eyes.

". . . and because of the kind of things you make me do, anything that comes into your head. The film is finished, understand?"

Tom just held out his hands in confusion. The Métro clamored into the station, blocking him from her sight, and Jeanne knew that was the end: the train would glide away with him in it, and that would be the end of that complication. She was thankful there was no time to experience either pleasure or pain. It was simply finished.

The Métro pulled out. Tom was gone.

She turned, and he was standing next to her.

"I'm tired of being raped!" she screamed.

They stalked each other like cats. Awkwardly, he swung at her, and the blow glanced ineffectually from her shoulders; she reared back and slashed at him with her purse. They skirmished like children in a sandbox, flailing wildly and cursing, and then, spent, they fell into each other's arms.

# Chapter
# Eleven

THE ALGERIAN seemed never to rest. The broken melodies from his saxophone suggested to Paul some creature in agony, mesmerized by the sound of its own lamentations. He was stretched out on the couch in his room, within view of the desk, the lamp turned low. The sickly green circle of the neon Ricard sign across the street seemed to mark the farthest limits of his world. Paul dozed.

He woke up suddenly, aware that a hand rested on his chest. In the half-light he recognized the solid silhouette of his mother-in-law, a shawl about her shoulders, perched on the edge of the chair.

"I can't sleep with that music," she said.

For an instant Paul imagined that she was Rosa. Her voice was similar, as was her touch.

"I came to this hotel just for one night," Paul said dreamily, "and I stayed five years."

"When Papa and I had this hotel, people came here to sleep."

There was no reproach in her voice, but Paul knew she disapproved.

"Now they do anything," he said, almost proudly. "They hide out, take drugs, play music . . ."

The weight of her hand on his chest was intolerable. The thought of human flesh in this narrow, sordid world—hers, his, and that of his hotel guests —disgusted him. There was something in her manner that went beyond an attempt to comfort.

"Remove that hand," he said.

But she thought she understood his isolation. He was, after all, Rosa's husband, and it was her duty to ease his pain. The contact soothed her, too. She was aware that Rosa had chosen what she considered to be a real man.

"You're not alone, Paul," she whispered, feeling the breadth of his chest. "I'm here."

He gently raised her hand and looked at it, and she felt a rush of gratitude. He moved it toward his lips, and then with sudden, brutal efficiency, he bit it.

Mère gasped, and began to claw at the chair to get away from him. She cradled the assaulted hand.

"You're insane," she cried. "I'm beginning to understand . . ."

She didn't finish the sentence, but Paul knew what she wanted to say—that he had driven Rosa to suicide. He had no objection to playing that role:

it was no more absurd than his present one of bereaved husband, secret lover, hotel clerk.

He leaped up from the couch.

"Do you want me to stop that music?" he asked, moving across the room toward the fuse box. "Okay, I'll make them shut up."

"What are you doing, Paul?" she asked fearfully.

"What's the matter, Mother, you upset?" He spoke in English, quickly and contemptuously. "Don't be upset, nothing to be upset about. You know, it takes so very little to make them afraid."

He pulled the circuit switch, and the whole *pension* lapsed into sudden darkness. She gasped and clung to the chair. Paul moved toward her.

"You want to know what they're afraid of?" he said loudly. "I'll tell you what they're afraid of. They're afraid of the dark, imagine that."

He took her roughly by the arm and led her toward the foyer.

"Come on, Mother. I want you to meet my friends."

"Lights," she said. "Lights!"

He pulled her toward the foot of the stairs. The sound of the saxophone had died a sudden death. The upper stories of the hotel filled with the sound of opening doors, shuffling feet, hushed voices speaking in several languages.

"I think you ought to meet a few clients of the hotel," Paul said with desperate irony, and he began to shout up the stairwell. "Hey, folks! I'd like you to say hello to Mom."

Someone struck a match on the second landing,

and Paul could see the ghostly, amorphous shapes massed there. Another match flared. He glimpsed faces he had seen for years—the human flotsam of which he was a part—grotesque and frail, and for their fear he despised them even more.

"Mom," he shouted, gesturing toward faces with one hand, gripping her arm with the other, "this is Mr. Juice-head Junkie here. And Mr. Saxophone, he's our connection, Mom, he gives us some hard stuff once in a while . . ."

She tried to pull away from him. "Let me go!" she gasped, but Paul held on.

". . . and right here is the beautiful Miss Best Blow-job of 1933! She still makes a few points when she takes out her teeth. Don't you want to say hello, Mom? This is Mom, everybody!"

The babble of languages grew stronger.

"The light, Paul," she pleaded. "Turn on the light."

"Oh, you afraid of the dark, Mom? She's afraid of the dark," he called up to the guests. "Aw, poor little thing. All right, sweetheart, I'll take care of you. Don't worry about it for a second."

Paul struck a match, and his own face shone ghastly from among the shadows. He laughed long and humorlessly, threw the match aside, and made his way back into the room. He restored the switch, and the lights came on. How easy it was to frighten them, he thought. They seemed equally afraid of being killed and of killing.

He stepped back into the foyer. The crowd in bathrobes and hastily donned raincoats dispersed, murmuring like dumb beasts. His mother-in-law still gripped the banister, watching him in utter disbelief.

A guest came in from the street carrying a roll of newspapers beneath one arm. He was older than Paul, but trim and distinguished-looking in his well-brushed overcoat and Tyrolean hat, which he promptly took off.

"Hello, Marcel," Paul said without emotion. He handed him his key.

Marcel nodded pleasantly to Paul's mother-in-law and climbed the stairs. She looked after him approvingly.

"Do you like him, Mother?" Paul asked.

She sensed some fresh trap, and was silent. He smiled sarcastically and shook his head. To him this was the night's final, crushing irony.

"Well," he said, "he was Rosa's lover."

# *Chapter*
# *Twelve*

Time HUNG suspended between the ornate stone façades of the Rue Jules Verne. Jeanne never turned into the street without first looking behind her, in case someone she knew might be watching. She had memorized the order of the parked cars. The café's bright, tattered awning and the deserted scaffolding across from the apartment building to which she returned again and again were totally familiar.

She welcomed the cold, stuffy gloom of the lobby. The concierge's window was closed, and the building appeared as deserted as ever. Jeanne stepped into the elevator and placed the portable record player she carried on the floor between her feet. Her anxiety about Paul mounted: as always, she wanted him, and feared to find him there. But their last encounter had ended so differently—so gently—that her anticipation ascended with her.

As she unlocked the apartment door, she thought she caught the same lilting, fading bar of music. The door swung open into what she thought were empty rooms. Her footsteps echoed off the tiles, and she could see half the circular room, and the mattress she knew so well, touched by sunlight. She called out, "Anybody here?" knowing there would be no answer.

She set the record player on the floor and turned toward the discarded furniture draped in the sheet. The shape was a bit frightening, and she addressed it playfully, trying to minimize her disappointment. "Something wrong? You have your problems, too, *hein?*"

Jeanne had not noticed that Paul lay in the far corner of the room, silent and inattentive. On the floor before him lay a partially eaten Camembert, a broken crust of bread, and a knife. He wore only trousers and an undershirt, his hair was disheveled, and the flesh about his eyes was dark from lack of sleep. He didn't even look up when he finally spoke. "There's butter in the kitchen."

Jeanne wheeled on him. "So you're here," she said, concealing her fright. "Why didn't you answer?"

"Go get the butter," he told her.

"I have to hurry. I have an appointment."

"Go get the butter!"

She looked at him in amazement. The day before

was forgotten. He now looked brutish, stretched on the unswept floor, propped up on one elbow, crumbs of bread clinging to his lips. He toyed with the cheese like some caged animal waiting to be fed.

Jeanne went into the kitchen and came back with the butter wrapped in tinfoil. She flung it down on the floor in front of him, and only that small violence seemed to get his attention. Paul looked at her with an expression of mild interest. It was her first act of defiance, but she wasn't strong enough to leave him.

"It makes me crazy," she said in her curious English, squatting cross-legged before him. "You're so damned sure I'll come back."

Paul just spread the butter on the remaining crust and ate it, chewing noisily. He tossed the bit of tinfoil aside and wiped his mouth with the back of his hand. He would do nothing to try to convince her to stay, but if she stayed, he would test her strength.

"What do you think," she asked ironically, speaking French, though she knew he preferred English, "that an American lying on the floor in an empty house, eating cheese and stale bread, is interesting?"

She tempted him, but he remained calm. The sight of him disgusted and at the same time excited her. She wondered why it was that his slovenliness appealed to her sexually, when it degraded and angered her, as did his contempt. Paul's anger and frustration had been mounting since the night before, and now he directed it toward her, indiscriminately. She was, after all, just a body—that was the idea of their pact.

Jeanne drummed her nails irritably on the floor. She tapped with her knuckles, producing a hollow sound.

"What's under here?" she said, knocking again. "It's a hollow space. Can you hear it?"

Paul roused himself and crawled forward. He rapped on the floor with his fist, then ran his fingernail along the edge of the carpet, loosening what seemed to be the cover of a hiding place.

"Don't open it," Jeanne said.

"Why not?"

"I don't know. Don't open it."

She grabbed Paul's wrist.

"What about that?" he said. "Can't I open it?"

He watched her, his interest growing. He could easily have opened the secret place, but he preferred to wait. Her resistance excited him.

"Now, wait a minute," he said, tearing her hand from his wrist. "Maybe there's jewels in it. Maybe there's gold."

Jeanne couldn't look at him. She didn't want him to open it, but she was reluctant to tell him why.

"You afraid?" he taunted. "You're always afraid."

Again he reached for the board.

"No," she said. "Maybe there's some family secrets inside."

Paul withdrew his hand.

"Family secrets?" he said, and his voice was deceptively docile. "I'll tell you about family secrets."

Paul grasped her neck in one hand, and her arm in the other, and forced her to lie face-down on the parquet floor. He felt unreasonable anger at her mention of the family—that great moral institution, he thought, untouchable divine creation, formed to breed virtue in good citizens, tabernacle of all virtues, and just incidentally, everything he most hated.

Jeanne struggled feebly. "What are you doing?" she asked, as he slipped his hand beneath her body and unbuttoned her jeans.

"I'm going to tell you about the family," he said, violently wrenching her trousers down around her knees, and baring her buttocks. "That holy institution, meant to breed virtue into savages."

Jeanne gasped for breath, struggling. Paul pinned her with the weight of his own body, one hand gripping the back of her neck. For a moment he seemed uncertain of what course to take, but then he saw the tinfoil wrapper containing the butter. With one foot he retrieved it.

"I want you to repeat after me," he said, digging the fingers of his free hand into the soft butter. Leisurely, he applied it to her anus, greasing her, he thought, like a pig for the skewer. His fingers were brutally efficient.

"No and no," she insisted, not really believing that he would go through with it. "No!"

Paul unfastened and stripped away his own trousers. He rose on his knees, still pressing against the back of Jeanne's neck, and forced his legs between hers. Jeanne felt herself being primed for

the assault, and she felt terror and utter helplessness.

"Now, repeat after me. Holy family . . ." he
began, spreading her buttocks with his strong fingers. He lay against her, probing for entrance.
"Come on, say it! Holy family, the church of good
citizens . . ."

"Church," she cried, ". . . good citizens."

She screamed, her face pressed against the smooth
boards, her eyes clamped shut. The pain was sudden and excruciating. His penis had become a
weapon.

"Say it!" he commanded, breathing heavily. "The
children are tortured until they tell their first
lie. . . ."

"The children . . ."

She cried out again as he forced himself deeper
into her.

"Where the will is broken by repression," he
said, the words hissing between his teeth.

"Where the will is broken . . ."

She began to sob, as much from humiliation as
pain. Paul only renewed his assault, his body seized
by an urgent, mounting rhythm. He was huge in
that virgin place.

"Where freedom is assassinated," he said.

"Freedom is . . ."

"Freedom is assassinated by egotism."

His fingers dug into her flesh, as if she might
evaporate and leave him stranded. There was no
escaping him now, and no denial, and her sobs only
seemed to propel him deeper.

"Family . . ."

"Family," she repeated in a long, dying wail.

"Your fucking, fucking family," he gasped, stiffening. "Oh, God, Jesus!"

Jeanne lay pinned to the floor, utterly helpless. Paul's spasm passed, but he didn't withdraw from her. He took her hair in one hand and turned her face toward the hollow spot in the floor. With the other hand he raised the board slightly.

"Open it!" he told her.

"Why?" Jeanne sobbed. What more could he want, after this ultimate degradation?

"Open it!" he said.

She raised the carpet, exposing a cavity in the floor no larger than the size of a brick. It was empty.

Paul tumbled from her and lay heaving on the floor. All orifices had now been violated, all were empty. His void remained unfilled.

Slowly Jeanne pulled on her pants, stifling her sobs, wiping her nose on the rough, woven sleeve of her peasant's blouse. She could have left him then, but she sensed that her own power was on the ascendancy. He had no right to brand her that way —like a slave.

She went into the hall and picked up her record player and carried it into the living room, where she knelt to open it. She unwound the wire, and taking the plug, inserted it into the old socket in the floor. Blue sparks spat at her, and she jerked her hand away, shocked.

*"Merde!"* she exclaimed.

She looked in at Paul, who seemed recovered,

one arm lying across his face. Jeanne remembered that she didn't know his name.

"Hey, you!" she called.

He turned toward her. "Yeah?" he said thickly.

"I've got a surprise for you."

"What?" Paul didn't understand, and she motioned to him, pretending to smile.

"I've got a surprise for you."

Paul raised himself to his knees and buttoned his trousers.

"That's good," he said. "I like surprises."

He had already dismissed what had gone before —just another temple to defile—and she hated him more for that dismissal than for the act. She wanted to hurt him, to short-circuit that powerful body, to see his strength drain away, to see some evidence of physical torment. She could barely wait.

"What is it?" Paul asked.

"Music," she said, still smilling. "But I don't know how to make it work."

She handed him the cord and pointed to the socket in the floor. Then she moved back. Paul gripped the plug, and without hesitation, forced it hard into the socket. There was a spray of sparks and a loud cracking noise as he jumped and flung away the cord.

"You enjoy that?" he asked, controlling himself.

Jeanne wasn't sure.

"You know," she said, "there's a cat that's got it in for me. He only comes when you're not here. The minute you leave, he'll come in. He'll look at me."

Her eyes filled with tears.

"Are you crying about the cat?" he asked, unmoved.

"I'm crying because I knew you'd get a shock, and I didn't say anything. I'm crying because of what you did. I'm crying because I can't take it anymore."

"That's a phrase for suicides," Paul said matter-of-factly. "Some of them even write that down. Are you going to kill yourself?"

"Why do you ask me that?"

"No particular reason." He paused. "You think about suicide at least once a day, right?"

"Not me. But I like the idea—it's romantic."

"I used to know someone who never seemed to think about it, and then committed suicide."

Jeanne jumped to her feet.

"Oh, my God," she said. "I forgot my appointment. I only came here to give you the record player."

"Appointments are for breaking."

She dried her tears on the sleeve of her coat and looked down at him. Paul hadn't moved.

"And you?" she asked, heading for the door.

"What about me?"

"Are you going to kill yourself?"

Paul smiled for the first time.

"I'm not the type who kills himself," he said. "I'm the type who kills."

# Chapter Thirteen

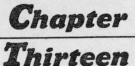

THE OLD barge listed heavily to starboard, its name—*L'Atalante,* like the old Vigo movie—barely discernible among the flakes of peeling ing paint on the prow. Jeanne had often passed it, moored in the Canal St. Martin, draped in strings of colored lights and displaying a sign above the cabin advertising it as a dance hall. The sign had toppled, the huge rusted cables seemed barely able to keep the barge afloat, and the foredeck was piled with bits of cheap furniture, lamp shades, and a few brass nautical fittings.

Jeanne hurried across the cobblestones of the quay. Tom and his crew waited patiently in the prow, and she waved. He seemed so harmless now, and so predictable, compared with Paul's unreasonable violence. Whatever Tom did, it was simply a game—a game of filmmaking—but with Paul things were never the same. Each time he pushed her farther, and there was no going back. It seemed that every time she met Tom, she brought with her a new and more extreme degradation that he would never even suspect. She was growing accustomed to this double life, though each time she left Paul, she told herself that it was the last time.

The barge captain stood among his junk, gripping a cigar in one heavily tattooed hand. "I won't sell anything," he told her as she came aboard.

"Everyone has something to sell," Jeanne said, smiling. Some of his scrap she could use in her little antique shop near Les Halles.

Tom came forward, took her by the arm, and gently led her to the railing in the prow. The cameraman shoved his hands into a black bag, hastily loading new film; the soundman squatted on the deck, preparing for the interview. He frowned when the captain put an old seventy-eight record on his phonograph, and a nasal masculine voice began to sing *"Parlami d'amore, Mariu,"* accompanied by much static.

Tom asked Jeanne, "What is your profession?"

"I'm a busybody."

She smiled for the camera.

"I thought you were an antique dealer," he said with a certain gravity.

"No, I'm in business with the twins. I'm the nosy one, I dig things up."

"What kind of things?"

"Everything from 1880 to 1935."

"Why just those years?"

"Because, in antiques, those years were revolutionary."

He looked at her in exasperation.

"I don't understand," he said. "Repeat, please. What kind of years were they?"

"Revolutionary. Yes, art nouveau is revolutionary in comparison with the rest of the nineteenth century and the Victorian era. Compared with bric-a-brac and bad taste."

"Bad taste?"

Tom looked around at the members of the crew, as if seeking some explanation; Jeanne obviously wasn't responding as he had planned.

"Taste?" he repeated. "What is that? And how can you feel revolutionary about collecting old things that once were revolutionary?"

"Do you want to fight?" she asked, realizing that he was taunting her.

"Okay, okay."

He raised his hands in acquiescence.

"Where do you find these . . . revolutionary objects?"

"At auctions, at different markets, in the country, in private homes . . ."

"You go into people's homes? What kind of people are these?"

"Old people," she said, "or else their sons, nephews, grandchildren. They wait for the old folks to die. And then they sell it all, as fast as they can."

"Isn't that a little morbid? Frankly, it disgusts

me a little. The smell of old things, the remains of the dead."

"No, it's exciting."

She paced the deck, enthusiastic now.

"The way I operate," she explained, "the past is exciting. It's a find—an object with a history. Listen, once I found the alarm clock of the executioner of Paris."

"That's disgusting. Would you like to have the hangman's alarm clock next to your bed?"

She stepped up to him, hands on her hips.

"Are you really trying to start a fight?" she asked. "Or do you simply have an aversion to antiques?"

"I listen to you peddle this old stuff, talk about that disgusting alarm clock . . ."

He paused, controlling the emotion in his voice, and went on.

"And then I see you—healthy, clean, modern . . ."

"Modern?" She laughed. "What does that mean? It's only fashion. Look around you. Dresses from the '30's or '40's . . ."

"Dresses I can understand. That makes me think of movies . . ."

He spread his arms, looking toward the sky.

". . . of stars when there really were stars. Rita Hayworth . . ."

Jeanne shook her head in disappointment.

"When it comes to movies," she said, "then you understand. Well, that's a way of refusing the present. I'm in the process of having a dress made like the one my mother wore in the photograph in 1946. She was beautiful, with those square shoulders—"

"Well," Tom interrupted, "that's a way of refusing the present."

"It's just a lot easier to love something that doesn't affect us too directly, something which keeps a certain distance. Like your camera."

It was a kind of indictment. Tom looked hurt, turned and spoke rapidly to the cameraman.

"Distances! You'll see . . . Give me the camera, I'll go on from here."

He told the soundman to hang up the microphone.

"Let it run. Now, beat it, all of you!" He shooed even the script girl away and turned angrily back to Jeanne. "I don't live on nostalgia. The present tense is something. Sit on that swing."

He pointed to an almost dilapidated swing constructed in the prow; she followed his instructions, impressed by his sudden show of initiative.

He talked while he focused the camera.

"Move a little. Sing."

Jeanne began to swing. She hummed the song, "Une jolie fille sur la balançoire," and played the part.

Tom laughed.

"That's something else," he said. "You know why I sent them away?"

"Because you're angry. Or because you want to be alone with me."

"And why do I want to be alone with you?"

"You have something to tell me," she speculated. "In private."

"Bravo!" shouted Tom. "What?"

"Is it happy or sad?"

"It's a secret."

"Then it's happy. What kind of a secret?"

"Let's see . . ."

He pretended to be thinking.

". . . a secret between a man and a woman . . ."

"Then it's obscene," she said, laughing. "Or it's about love."

"Yes, love. But that's not all."

"A secret about love."

She rested her chin on her fist; Tom continued to press his eye to the camera viewer.

"A secret about love with something that's not love in it," she said. "You've got me."

"I wanted to tell you that, a week from now, I'm going to marry you."

"How about that!"

"Naturally, it depends on you."

"And you?"

"I've decided," he said. "Everything's ready . . ."

"Oh, Tom, all of this is so bizarre. It seems impossible."

"The shot's a bit shaky. My hands are trembling with emotion."

She began to swing back and forth, raising her feet higher each time.

"You haven't answered yet," he called out.

"Because I don't understand any of it."

Her face was deeply flushed, her smile broad and uncompromising. She looked around her—at the canal, the captain packing his junk in boxes, the houses lining the quay, the bare plane trees, the synchronized flight of a pair of pigeons—and could concentrate on nothing. Slowly the swing came to a halt.

"Well?" said Tom. "Yes or no?"

A trace of anxiety passed across her face; she put her arms around his neck.

"Stop shooting," she whispered. "I'm supposed to marry you, not the camera."

Tom picked up an old life preserver, and in celebration, hurled it out into the water of the canal; to their surprise, it promptly sank.

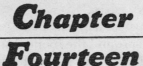

# Chapter
# Fourteen

JEANNE opened the door to her mother's apartment with her own key. She had run up the stairs instead of taking the elevator, anxious to convey the good news; the sight of their expansive, comfortably furnished sitting room had a slight dampening effect upon her. Primitive African weapons and art objects similar to those hanging in the villa covered one wall. The room was bright and airy, but conveyed a sense of nostalgia and time lost.

She ran into her mother's room.

A handsome woman with carefully styled, graying hair and an innate air of authority stood over the bed, which was cluttered with old army uniforms.

She held a pair of well-preserved, highly polished boots against her bosom.

"H'lo, Mother," Jeanne said, hugging her.

"You're back early."

"Uh-huh, just so happens I am."

She strutted around the room, casually inspecting the gold braid on one of the uniforms, touching the heels of the boots.

"I'm in a very good mood," she said.

"Good."

Her mother held up the boots admiringly.

"Tell me. What do you think? Shall I send them out to the villa?"

"Send everything."

She pirouetted in the middle of the floor, arms raised, flung the hair out of her face.

"Olympia's the museum of the family, anyway."

"But not the boots," her mother insisted. "I'll keep them here with me. It makes me shiver just to touch them."

Jeanne picked up a round cap encrusted with braid, set it at an angle on her head; she picked up a heavy wool uniform in drab and ran her hand over the epaulets and the gold buttons.

"Uniforms," she said. "All those military things never age."

She discarded the coat and cap. Her father's old regulation military pistol lay exposed in the bureau drawer; she took it from the worn holster and inspected it. The cartridges were still in place.

"It used to seem so heavy when I was little and Papa was teaching me to shoot it."

She aimed it at the potted vine hanging in the window.

"Why don't you send it?" she asked her mother. "What are you going to do with a gun?"

"In any respectable household, a firearm is always useful."

She began to pack the uniforms into the open suitcases.

Jeanne replaced the pistol, shut the drawer; she began to rummage through a box of old papers.

"You don't even know how to hold it," she said.

"The important thing is to have it. It has its own effect."

Jeanne discovered a cracked red-leather wallet in the box. She turned her back to her mother, opened it, and pulled out the Colonel's old identity card. Then she discovered a photograph hidden underneath the card, yellow and cracked; it was of a young Arab girl, proudly displaying her bare breasts to the camera.

Jeanne hid the wallet in her purse. She turned to her mother and showed her the photograph.

"And her?" she asked. "Who is she?"

Her mother's frown was almost imperceptible. Obviously this had been one of the Colonel's many mistresses during his African campaigns.

"Fine example of a Berber," she said with dignity, as she continued to pack. "A strong race. I tried to keep several in the house, but they make terrible domestics."

She was the female counterpart of the successful

professional soldier—a model of perfection and stoicism under stress. Now her duty was to the revered memory of her gallant husband. She would let nothing sully it.

She closed a suitcase decisively and set it on the floor. She smiled at her daughter.

"I'm glad I decided to send all that to the country. Things keep piling up."

Jeanne kissed her affectionately.

"Soon you'll have all the room you want."

Her mother looked at her, but Jeanne turned and walked to the door.

"I've got to go," she said. "I haven't finished working. I just stopped by to tell you . . ."

She stepped out onto the landing, and her mother followed. Jeanne leaned on the button for the elevator.

"Tell me what?" her mother asked.

"That I'm getting married."

She opened the elevator door and stepped inside.

"You're what?"

Her mother gripped the ornate elevator cage, staring at her incredulously.

"I'm getting married in a week," called Jeanne as she dropped from sight.

On her way to the shop, Jeanne stepped into an automatic photo machine in the Bir Hakeim Métro station. She pushed the coins into the slot, pulled the string on the short plastic curtain, and found herself alone on a hard wooden bench facing her own reflection in the two-way mirror.

The flashbulb fired. She turned her face to the

right, then to the left, waiting each time for the automatic camera to photograph her.

Impulsively she unbuttoned her blouse and thrust her exposed breasts toward the lens.

"Fine example of a Berber," she said to herself as the last flash fired.

Waiting on the Métro platform, Jeanne stared down into the narrow, cluttered street, watching people move furtively past the café, some of them carrying valises—travelers from St. Lazare, she thought absently, many of them foreigners. She touched the Berber photograph in her pocket, and the one she had just made of herself. The first one had told her something about her father she had never suspected; now she thought of him as a man capable of sexual desire, and of inspiring it. Even he must have had a secret life, and the idea intrigued her. If her mother had known, she no longer cared. How quickly people accommodated themselves to the demands of flesh. By having herself photographed with her breasts bared, she felt she had established a new relationship with her father. She had also done it as a joke, she told herself, and she wanted to share it with one of her lovers. Then she realized that both Tom and Paul would disapprove, but for different reasons: Tom would call her vulgar, and Paul would torture her for her sentimentality.

Jeanne boarded the train and rode across town thinking of her adventure, ignorant of the other passengers. The idea that her father might have had an affair seemed to justify her encounters with

Paul. But if she was really going to marry Tom, she would have to make some adjustment, at least in her own mind, or something disastrous would result.

She left the train and walked past the shell of the old Les Halles market to her antique shop. The first thing she noticed was that her windows needed washing. The single room was a jungle: lamp stands, hat racks, the spindly legs of upturned chairs, and a settee massed with dusty bottles. A barrel full of old walking sticks stood next to the door.

In the rear of the shop, her helpers—Monique and Mouchette—were unpacking a box of junk. Twins, they both wore their tangled blond hair long, and their jeans were covered with bright patches. Technically they were Jeanne's assistants. She had started the shop with money from her mother, but it was mostly the twins who confronted the rich matrons from Auteuil who came to buy Jeanne's relics. They were younger than Jeanne, but because they had participated in the student revolt of 1968 while still in grade school, they tended to treat her like an impetuous younger sister.

"Hello," Jeanne called. "I'm getting married."

The twins straightened up and pushed their hair from their eyes. They looked at Jeanne in disbelief, and then at each other.

"What's it going to be like married?" Monique asked.

She knew they did not approve of Tom.

"I'll be calmer, more organized," Jeanne said, unbuttoning her coat. She planned to help with the unpacking and pricing, like the responsible proprietor she wished she could be. "I've decided to get serious."

The twins merely laughed.

"What would you do in my place?" Jeanne asked.

"I'd hit myself over the head," Mouchette said.

"I'd become a nun," said Monique.

And give up sex? Jeanne thought. She started to slip out of her coat, then paused. She would begin by telling Paul that she was to be married, that their adventure was over. After all, her parents' marriage had endured, probably because of just such self-denial on her father's part. For the moment she felt terribly strong.

"I've made a major decision," she said, buttoning her coat again. "It's over. I'll never see him again after today."

"No wedding?" called Mouchette.

"Yes," said Jeanne over her shoulder. "I'm getting married. I'm a free woman!"

Monique and Mouchette exchanged glances, more confused than ever.

"I'll never understand her," said Monique.

"In any case," Mouchette said, "you don't say 'free,' you say 'liberated.'"

# Chapter
## Fifteen

A FREE woman! Jeanne turned the phrase over in her mind as she left the shop. Self-absorbed, she did not notice the panel truck parked at the curb.

Inside the truck, concealed behind stacks of cartons, knelt Tom and his crew, crowded together with sound equipment and the Arriflex, and a jumble of wires. Tom pressed the camera to his eye, focusing on Jeanne as she ran toward the corner. The script girl, her hair tied up in a scarf, knelt beside him, their shoulders touching, but Tom was absorbed in his quarry.

"If I were in Jeanne's place," the script girl said, "I'd forget about the wedding, after a number like this."

Tom shifted position for a better view. The motor started with a loud blast, but the driver waited to see if Jeanne would hail a cab from the corner.

"You're acting like a private eye," the script girl told Tom.

He didn't answer, but moved his hand up over her sweater until it covered her small, firm breast. He pinched it playfully. "Maybe you'd like to be in her place," he said, without taking his eye from the camera.

Jeanne turned the corner and began walking up the street.

The driver followed closely, then pulled abreast of her. Tom hefted the Arriflex to his cameraman, making motions for him to begin filming. They were silent now, and intent.

Traffic halted at the light. Suddenly Jeanne turned and headed directly for the truck.

"She's seen us," said Tom. "We're screwed."

She came closer. Tom ducked, waving his crew down behind him. Aside from filming, he had a motive for following Jeanne, though he didn't like to admit it, even to himself. For the last few days he thought she had behaved strangely—arriving late, leaving abruptly, fighting in a Métro station. Something was wrong.

A door slammed next to the truck. Tom cautiously peered out the window. Jeanne was seated in the back seat of a taxi.

"Not screwed, after all," he said.

The taxi pulled off.

"Keep your distance," Tom told his driver. "She must not see us."

The taxi stopped at the next light. Jeanne leaned over the front seat and gave instructions to the driver. She had no idea that just a few feet from her hovered the lens of a camera. The light changed, and the truck took up its position behind the taxi.

Jeanne was oblivious of the outside world. She opened her purse and took out her makeup kit. She brushed her eyelashes with mascara, and precisely outlined her mouth with magenta lipstick.

Her taxi stopped within view of the ornate railway bridge leading into Passy. It was crowded with afternoon commuters spilling from the Métro station, and she wondered vaguely if Paul were among them. She got out, and paid the driver hurriedly, and then started across the street in the direction of the Viaduc Café and the Rue Jules Verne's familiar façades.

Tom and his crew knelt together, their faces pressed against the tiny window.

"Where are we?" he asked, watching as Jeanne passed the café.

"The Rue Jules Verne," the driver said. "In the seventh arrondissement."

"The mystery is complete." Tom shrugged his shoulders and instructed the cameraman to keep filming. The possibility that Jeanne might be on her way to another lover occurred to him.

"All right," he said nervously. "Now pass her."

Jeanne had almost reached the apartment building with the high iron gate. The truck pulled ahead of her.

The street was just as it always was, sedate and almost empty of passing cars. The scaffolding across the street loomed like the skeleton of some prehistoric beast, and the distant rattle of the Métro reached Jeanne. She paused next to the door of opaque yellow glass.

The truck stopped and sat with the motor idling.

Jeanne turned toward the door of the apartment building. Something in the street caught her eye—a panel truck. The back door was slightly open. A long, dark cylinder protruded from the crack between the doors: the shotgun mike. She recognized it instantly. She now had to make a choice.

Panic and anger gave way to a scheme. She turned and continued up the street.

"Are you sure she hasn't seen you?" Tom asked the soundman.

"It's practically impossible," he said, drawing the mike almost out of sight, as the truck rolled slowly forward again.

"Do your best," Tom said. "Just try to get her footsteps, and some of the mood."

Jeanne felt like screaming. She wanted to attack Tom, she wanted to fly away and never be bothered again. By now the truck seemed so conspicuous that she wanted to laugh or make obscene gestures. But that would suit Tom's purpose. It would be better to deceive him, and in such a way that he couldn't fail to understand.

She paused on the next corner. Across the street stood a Romanesque church, the stone dark with soot and age. Without looking right or left, she crossed to it and slipped behind the heavy wooden door.

"Stop!" Tom told the driver, and turned to his crew. "No sound!"

He swung open the doors and jumped into the street. "On tiptoe now," he cautioned, as the others scrambled out behind him. Tom felt that he had discovered the essence of Jeanne at last. It would never have occurred to him that she was religious. The idea pleased him. It confirmed her purity.

The church was gloomy and almost deserted. A bank of flickering candles filled one alcove. The altar was illuminated only by the dying light of day, filtered through somber stained glass high above the chapel. The cameraman raised the Arriflex to his eye, and following Tom's hand signals, filmed the stained-glass windows and then swept down through the nave, searching for Jeanne.

She was kneeling in a confessional, her hands clasped in prayer.

"Zoom in on her," Tom instructed, and he and the others crept forward. They moved closer, until they could plainly hear her words.

"You're a bastard, Tom," she said, her eyes focused straight ahead. "You're a bastard, a bastard. A *bastard!* I loathe you, I hate you."

Tom stumbled closer, unable to believe what he

was hearing. He stood next to her, wanting an explanation, but unable to speak. She continued her litany, without ever raising her eyes.

The script girl came forward and took Tom by the arm. "That's enough," she whispered.

"You're right," he said. "She really screwed me."

The crew followed him outside. No one spoke as they clambered back into the truck and unloaded their equipment. Tom felt foolish, angry.

The truck jerked forward and rumbled up the Rue Jules Verne.

The nave grew darker. An unfelt breeze stirred the candle flames. For several minutes Jeanne didn't move. She knew she had made Tom suffer, but he deserved it. For an instant she thought she would cry from frustration: she had missed her chance of finding Paul at the apartment.

She exited into the cold winter evening, wondering if she would ever see him again.

# Chapter
## Sixteen

THE HOTEL was quiet for once. Paul locked the front door, after looking up the street toward the café, and then turned down the lamp—a routine that was totally familiar and increasingly tedious. He considered the satisfaction he would derive from locking all of his guests out, instead of in. The fact was that he no longer cared about the money. He felt horribly alone. Rosa's body was to be delivered from the autopsist's the next day. No doubt, he thought, that he and her mother would derive grim pleasure from the homecoming.

He returned to his room, took a bottle of Jack Daniels from his wardrobe closet, and poured himself a drink. His hand was steady as he tossed it back, but his guts were roiled and cold. He took his bathrobe from the closet and put it on, jerking the sash tight about his stomach. The room contained nothing else that seemed to pertain to him—the books and pictures were all Rosa's, since Paul wanted no relics—but he felt sheltered there, and reluctant to leave. Marcel had asked him up to his own room, an odd invitation. He always referred to Marcel, with bitter humor, as his wife's unaccredited lover. That made it sound somehow more hopeless, and callous. Of course he had also had his lovers—barmaids, dreary shopgirls, whatever bodies came his way—mostly out of habit. But Rosa seemed to have something else in mind. As her official lover, Paul thought he was entitled to certain privileges, among them love. How presumptuous he had been.

He knew it had taken courage for Marcel to invite him up. How many nights had Paul sat in this room, waiting and watching the green neon Ricard sign across the street, while Rosa was with her lover. Well, Paul told himself, if Marcel waxed sloppy and sentimental tonight, he might just have to shove Marcel's head through one of the cheap pasteboard walls. On the other hand, there was a chance Marcel could tell him something of interest.

Paul climbed the stairs and knocked on Marcel's door.

*"Entre!"* The response was polite and immediate.

Paul entered a narrow room cluttered with books and magazines and filled with a warm glow from the lamp's crimson shade. The walls were hung with Lautrec and Chagall prints, photographs of idealized natural landscapes torn from *Paris Match,* used race-track tickets, letters, clippings, and a poster of Albert Camus. Marcel sat at a desk strewn with copies of *Le Monde, Paris-Soir,* and half a dozen other newspapers, cutting out an article with a pair of long shears. He, too, wore a bathrobe.

"I didn't come here to cry with you," Paul told him.

Marcel continued to ply the shears. His self-control annoyed Paul.

"Does it bother you if I keep working?" Marcel asked. "It distracts me after what happened."

He saw that Paul compared their bathrobes. Both were of the same tartan-plaid fabric.

"Identical," Marcel said, with some satisfaction. "Rosa wanted our bathrobes to be exactly alike."

Paul's irritation increased. He didn't know about the bathrobes, and found them ridiculous. "You can't tell me anything I don't already know," he said, lying. He decided to take the initiative, and began to poke at a neat pile of clippings on the desk. "I was wondering why you save these. Is it a job, or a hobby?"

"I don't like the word 'hobby,' " Marcel retorted. "It's a job to round out my salary."

"Then it's serious." Paul mocked him. "It's a job that makes you read. Very instructive."

"Be sincere," Marcel said. "Didn't you know that we had identical bathrobes?"

Paul laughed, but the sound was hollow.

"We have lots of things in common," Marcel went on, but Paul interrupted him.

"I know everything. Rosa often told me about you."

In the presence of another man, even one as fastidious as Marcel Paul could sentimentalize about his wife, without the feeling of impotent rage. Marcel was a man, and had never been a threat, except perhaps in the way Rosa used him.

"Would you like a shot of bourbon?" he asked Marcel, in a sudden impulse toward generosity. He stepped to the door.

"Wait." Marcel opened a desk drawer and took out his own bottle of Jack Daniels. "I have some of my own."

"Is that another present from Rosa?"

"I don't much care for it, but Rosa always wanted it around. I've often wondered if by these details we can explain, understand together . . ."

Paul accepted a glass of whiskey.

"For almost a year, Rosa and I . . ." Marcel stumbled over his words. "Regularly, but without passion," he said, deciding to leave the sex act unspecified. "I thought I knew her as well as one can know one's . . ."

"Mistress," Paul said casually.

"But awhile ago something happened which I couldn't explain."

Marcel pointed to a wedge of white wall near the ceiling, where the paper had been ripped away.

"Rosa climbed up on the bed," he said, "and tried to tear off the paper with her hands. I stopped her—she was ruining her nails. She did it with a strange violence. I had never seen her like that."

Some realization was nagging at Paul. "Our room was painted white," he said. "She wanted it different from the others in the hotel, to make it seem like a normal home. She wanted to change it here, too, and she began with the walls."

Paul sat heavily on the bed. How easy it was for someone to set up another life. He thought of Jeanne, and of the fact that they did not know each other's names. Was it possible that Rosa had also created with Marcel her bleakest vision of existence? And that vision was an exact duplicate of her real life with Paul. For a moment Paul couldn't speak. He looked at Marcel with fascination.

"You must have been a good-looking man," he said.

Marcel sat on the bed beside him. "Not as much as you."

"You're in good shape." Paul patted him through the bathrobe. "What do you do for the belly? That's where I have a problem."

"Ah, I have a secret," Marcel said, but he didn't finish. "Why did Rosa betray you with me?" he asked Paul abruptly.

Paul looked into his guileless eyes: this man would never understand.

"You don't think Rosa killed herself?" Paul asked quietly.

"It's difficult for me to believe it."

Marcel seemed frightened by the admission. He got up and walked to the window, grasped a bar wedged in the frame, and began to chin himself.

"This is the secret for my stomach," he called.

Paul just stared at him, the reconstruction of himself. Rosa had dressed him like Paul, made his favorite drink the same booze. Paul had searched for a letter from Rosa, had found nothing but her inconsequential and sometimes obscene mementos. Now he realized that Marcel and Marcel's room were the message he sought. It was like looking in the mirror. The banality of it all was overwhelming.

He walked to the door and paused. "In all sincerity," he said to Marcel, "I wonder what she saw in you."

# Chapter
# Seventeen

THE CAVERNS of Les Halles seemed untouched by the morning sunlight, the windows up beneath the eaves draped in shadow, and backed by the darkness of an enormous silent room. Untold thousands of animal carcasses had passed beneath that roof—Jeanne had often seen the legions of marbled meat marshaled on steel hooks—and now the building was itself doomed and scheduled for destruction. It had, she thought, viewing it from just inside the door of a shop on the Rue de la Cossonnerie, become its own funeral parlor. But she had no time for such macabre thoughts; death was something that could not touch her, especially today, when she was the focal point of the bridal shop, and dressed in antique satin, her curls piled

upon her head, where she held them, the single
red rose Tom has presented her clasped in one
hand, turning slowly for his appraisal.

The Arriflex rested on the pavement outside,
secure on its tripod, because there was no room in
the tiny shop. The cameraman bent to the view-
finder, concentrating, while the soundman knelt
before his tape recorder, testing the microphone.
Tom danced behind the camera, waiting for the
filming to start, his brightly patterned scarf trailing
from his neck in a slightly self-conscious display of
enthusiasm. The woman who owned the shop, rec-
ognizing the certainty of a sale, had tried to convince Jeanne to choose the more expensive wedding
gown in *peau-de-soie*, but she prefered the more
traditional style, though her gown was secondhand,
and torn beneath one arm. The thrust of her breast
was visible through the tear, firm and virginal.

She became impatient with Tom's preparations,
and she wanted him to begin while she was able to
suspend her own disbelief. He noticed her dis-
comfort.

"Inspiration isn't like a light turning on," he
called.

"Then what kind of a director are you?"

"You can't buy ideas like sausage!" He turned
to his crew. "Are you ready? *On tourne . . .*"

Jeanne watched Tom take the microphone and
confront the camera to make his introduction,
stepping jauntily from one foot to the other. He
was, she decided, as incurably romantic as herself.

"We're at Les Halles," he began, while the camera ground away. "In these old stores are dresses, dresses waving gently in the breeze—a sensation of white. They are wedding dresses . . ."

He waved the soundman forward and shouted, "Action!"

Jeanne found that Tom was kneeling before her, so as not to block the shot, and holding the mike at the level of her breasts.

"How do you see marriage?" he asked.

She felt the movement of air, knew it was not a breeze, but wind. Clouds had massed to the north. Warm air in winter, she reflected, always meant rain.

"I see it everywhere," she said. "Always."

"Everywhere?" Tom asked.

"On walls, on house fronts."

"On walls? On house fronts?"

Tom already sounded disappointed. She wondered if they really had any chance together, when she felt stifled just trying on her wedding gown.

"Yes," she said, confronting the camera. "On posters. And what do the posters say? What do they sell?"

"They talk about cars, canned meat, cigarettes . . ." Tom suggested.

"No. The subject is the young couple before marriage, without children. Then we see them after the marriage, with children. The posters are about marriage, even if they don't say so. The ideal, successful marriage isn't in the old style anymore, in church, with a depressed husband and a complaining wife. Today, the advertised marriage is smiling."

"Smiling?"

"Of course. And why not take these marriages as seen in advertising seriously? It's the pop marriage."

"Pop!" For Tom it was a revelation. He had never thought of marriage in those terms. "That's an idea," he said. "For pop youth, a pop marriage. But what if the pop marriage doesn't work?"

"Fix it like a car," Jeanne said. "The couple are like two workmen in overalls, repairing a motor."

"And in the case of adultery, what happens?" Tom pressed.

The shopwoman completed her fitting and stepped back, her hands raised in appreciation.

"In the case of adultery," Jeanne said, "there are three or four workmen, instead of two."

"And love? Is love pop, too?"

Tom knelt at her feet, his head resting among the folds of *peau-de-soie* draped over the little divan. He looked at Jeanne adoringly.

"No," she decided. "Love is not pop."

"If it's not pop, what is it?"

Jeanne noticed that the crew enjoyed their exchange, and she wondered if they suspected something Tom didn't. Behind them, the sky grew darker.

"The workmen go to a secret place," she said. "They take off their overalls, becoming men and women again, and they make love."

Tom was delighted. He jumped to his feet and cried, "You're superb! You even look superb!"

"It's the dress that makes the bride," Jeanne offered modestly.

"You're better than Rita Hayworth," Tom gushed, using his catalog of film comparisons. "Better than Joan Crawford, Kim Novak, Lauren Bacall, Ava Gardner when she loved Mickey Rooney!"

These names had nothing to do with her. She tried to believe in herself as a bride, but she couldn't —at least not Tom's bride, not now. She wanted to tear the gown away, to be away from his childish adoration and the eyes of the camera, the crew, and the woman who had stepped to close the door because the rain had started.

"What are you doing?" Tom called. "Stop!" He pushed the door open again and told the cameraman to keep filming. But the rain fell harder, and the script girl was the first to run for cover. The cameraman took off his jacket and threw it over the Arriflex. The soundman began to gather his equipment under the awning next door.

"Why aren't you filming in the rain?" Tom shouted. "Why are you stopping?"

The bottom seemed to fall out of the sky. Tom rushed into the street to help move the camera, as the shouts of dismay were drowned out by the pounding rain. Jeanne moved cautiously toward the door, the gown gathered in her hands. She had a sudden, irresistible urge to see Paul, to be secure within the circular walls of the apartment, stripped of the gown and all other obligations. She hesitated, and then ran out into the downpour and up the Rue de la Cossonnerie, the rain instantly soaking her hair and the thin satin, cold but electrifying. She felt like singing, and she opened her mouth to the deluge.

No one but the shopowner saw Jeanne's escape. The woman still stood with her mouth open when Tom slipped back into the shop, soaking wet, and confronted the empty fitting platform.

"Jeanne," he said. "Where's Jeanne?"

"I don't know," the woman gasped. "She just jumped up and left."

"In the rain?"

"In the rain. In her wedding gown."

Together they peered out the door. The Rue de la Cossonnerie was deserted, backed by the outline of Les Halles, obscured by the rain.

# *Chapter*
# *Eighteen*

**P**AUL STOOD in the shelter of the railway bridge, looking up past the petals of blue-gray iron supporting the Métro, at the rainwater blowing from the arches out over the river. He held his overcoat about him, not because he was cold or wet— he had gained the bridge before the rain broke— but because he liked the feeling of strict containment. His hair had not been combed that morning, and the encroaching bald spot was more apparent. He seemed older than before, and more vulnerable. Today Rosa was to be brought to the room her mother had so carefully prepared for her, and Paul was on his way to another room, to meet another body that was very much alive, if nameless and without other significance for him. It occurred to him that the situation wasn't without humor, but he didn't laugh.

At that moment, a taxi stopped on the Rue Jules Verne, and Jeanne stepped out. She was completely soaked, and seemed almost naked. The thin satin had become transparent, assuming the color of her flesh, and it clung provocatively to the contours of her breasts and buttocks, and exposed even the light patch of pubic hair. Her curls were plastered to her face with rain. The cabdriver stared at her with dumb appreciation as she ran across the pavement and into the apartment building.

The rain slacked, and Paul dashed from his cover, bound for the Rue Jules Verne.

Jeanne hadn't brought her key, and she rushed to the concierge's window. The woman sat with her back to the foyer. "I beg your pardon," Jeanne said, raising her voice to be heard over the tattoo of driving rain, but the woman didn't turn around. A clap of thunder shook the building. Jeanne backed away from the window and sat on the wooden bench next to the elevator. She hugged her body, shivering.

It was there Paul saw her, and he experienced a new elation, knowing that she had come to him in such haste and abandon. The sound of his footsteps aroused her, but when Jeanne looked up expectantly, Paul passed her without a word and stepped into the elevator. They confronted each other through the elaborate scrollwork.

"Forgive me," Jeanne said. "Do you still want me?"

Paul didn't know why he should forgive her, and didn't care. He simply nodded his head and swung open the elevator door.

*"J'ai voulu te quitter, je n'ai pas pu,"* she said in a rush, and then remembered that he preferred English. "I wanted to leave you, but I couldn't. I can't!"

Paul said nothing. He gazed at her body—the dark circles of her nipples beneath the wet material, the outline of her narrow hips, the fullness of her thighs. Even the soft down of her legs showed through the satin, as if it were a second skin.

The elevator began to rise.

"I wanted to leave," she said again. "Do you understand?"

Still Paul didn't speak, his eyes moving up and down over her body. Jeanne began to raise the hem of the gown, leaning back against the cage, watching his face for signs of pleasure. Her calves and knees were revealed, then her thighs, then her pubic hair. She paused, then raised the gown higher, displaying a child's navel. The elevator rose higher.

"What else do you want from me?" she asked, grateful and exposed.

He might not have heard. Her words meant nothing, compared with her presence. He moved his hand forward and slipped his fingers between her legs, where she was moist and warm. She hesitated, then reached across and unfastened his trousers, and moved her hand among the maze of his clothing until she held him, firmly and unequivocally. Their arms formed a cross.

The elevator sighed as it reached its destination.

"*Voilà!*" shouted Paul, swinging open the door of the apartment. He began to sing, "There once was a man, and he had an old sow . . ."

Rain poured through the open window in the circular room, and he slammed it shut and turned toward her with a theatrical bow. Jeanne stood in the middle of the floor, shivering and laughing.

"You know, you're wet," he said, and he took her in his arms. The soaked gown was slick as ice, and her hair left a damp impression on his chest. He went into the bathroom for a towel.

Jeanne felt like a celebration. She was now his bride, and this was their honeymoon, and she turned around in the middle of the floor—just as she had the first day—and then threw herself down on the mattress. She hugged the pillow like an excited schoolgirl, and turned expectantly toward the door, waiting for Paul to reappear. It was then that her hand touched something damp behind the pillow. Jeanne sat up and jerked the pillow away. A dead rat lay on the sheet, blood dried about its mouth, its fur matted and wet.

She began to scream.

Paul arrived with the towel, which he dropped in her lap.

"A rat," he said matter-of-factly, but she clung to him, whimpering.

"It's only a rat," he repeated, amused by her

irrational fear. "There are more rats in Paris than people."

Paul reached down and picked the rat up by its tail, letting its head dangle before his face. Jeanne gasped and backed away. She was terrified and sickened by the sight and the touch of it, and she watched in disgust as Paul raised the carcass and opened his own mouth.

"Yum, yum, yum," he said, smacking his lips.

"I want to go," she stammered.

"Hey, wait. Don't you want a bite first? Don't you want something to eat?"

His cruelty was as exhausting as it was sudden.

"This is the end," she said.

"No, this is the end," he joked, pointing at the tail. "But I like to start with the head, that's the best part. Now, are you sure you won't have any? Okay . . ."

He lowered the rat's head to within an inch of his mouth. She turned away in horror.

"What's the matter?" he asked, needling her. "Don't you dig rats?"

"I want to go. I can't make love in this bed anymore, I can't. It's disgusting, nauseating." She shivered.

"Well," he said, "we'll fuck on the radiator, or standing on the mantel."

He turned toward the kitchen. "Listen," he called, dangling the rat. "I've got to get some mayonnaise for this, because it really is good with mayonnaise. I'll save the asshole for you."

He went into the kitchen, laughing loudly. "Rat's asshole with mayonnaise!"

"I want to leave, I want to get out of here," she shouted, unable to look even at the bed. How quickly the mood had changed; there was no predicting what he might do next. The desire she felt for him, and her own burgeoning passion, had evaporated at the touch of that dead, matted fur. For the first time she saw the room in all its sordidness. The odor of sex now reminded her of death. Her own audacity at being there frightened her.

"I can't take it anymore," she mumbled to herself. "I'm going away, I'm never coming back. Never."

She turned to go, just as Paul returned. He had disposed of the rat.

"*Quo vadis,* baby?" he asked playfully. He moved ahead of her into the hall, and bolted the front door. Jeanne looked at him with combined disgust and gratitude. She didn't really want to leave.

"Someone did it on purpose," she said, looking at Paul suspiciously. "I can feel it. It's a warning—it's the end."

"You're crazy."

"I should have told you right away." She wanted to challenge that overweening masculine assurance. "I've fallen in love with someone."

"Oh, isn't that wonderful?" Paul said mockingly. He stepped forward and ran his hands over the smooth material of her gown, probing her as he might a ripe avocado. "You know, you're going to have to get out of these wet duds."

"I'm going to make love with him," she insisted.

Paul ignored her. "First you have to take a hot bath, 'cause if you don't, you're going to get pneumonia. Right?"

He gently led Jeanne into the bathroom, and stooped to turn on both faucets full force. Then he took the hem of her gown, and began to lift it slowly, revealing her as she had revealed herself in the elevator.

"You get pneumonia," he said, "and then you know what happens? You die."

Jeanne raised her arms, and Paul pulled the gown over her head and discarded it behind him.

"And then you know what happens?"

She stood before him, naked, shaking her head.

"I get to fuck the dead rat!" he said.

"Ohhh," she moaned, burying her face in her hands. She knew he would never let her forget it.

Paul began to sing again. He rolled up his sleeves, then took Jeanne by the arm and led her gently into the tub. The water was beautifully warm. She sat in it slowly, feeling the chill and the anxiety draining out of her. Paul perched on the edge of the tub.

"Give me the soap," he said.

He grasped her ankle, and raised her foot until

it was on a level with his face. Slowly he began to soap her toes, the arch of her foot, then her calf. She was surprised at the softness of his touch. She felt that her limbs were made of elastic, as the steam rose between them, giving her skin a warm glow.

"I'm in love," she repeated.

Paul did not want to hear it. He ran his soapy hand down the inside of her thigh until it could go no farther. There he began to work up a lather.

"You're in love," he said with mock enthusiasm. "How delightful!"

"I'm in love," she insisted, and began to moan. His hand was relentless, and she rested her head against the enamel and closed her eyes.

"I'm in love, do you understand?" She gasped, but continued. "You know, you are old. And you're getting fat."

Paul released her leg, and it fell heavily into the water.

"Fat, is it? How unkind."

He soaped her neck and shoulders, moved his hand down toward her breasts. Jeanne was determined to make him take her seriously. She also felt an advantage that was new to her. She looked at him closely, and realized that what she was saying was true.

"Half your hair is out," she said, "and the other half is nearly white."

Paul smiled down at her, though her words

angered him. He soaped her breasts, then cupped one in his hand and regarded its magnitude critically.

"You know," he said, "in ten years you're going to be playing soccer with your tits. What do you think about that?"

Jeanne just raised her other leg, and Paul dutifully washed that one, too.

"And you know what I'm going to be doing?" he asked, his hand sliding downward again along the soft, slick skin of her inner thigh.

"You'll be in a wheelchair," Jeanne said, gasping when his fingers touched her clitoris.

"Well, maybe. But I think I'll be smirking and giggling all the way to eternity."

He released her leg, but Jeanne kept it thrust into the air. "How poetic. But please, before you get up, wash my foot."

*"Noblesse oblige."*

He kissed her foot, and then applied the soap.

"You know," Jeanne went on, "he and I, we make love."

"Oh, really." Paul laughed aloud, amused by the idea of being taunted by such a revelation. "That's wonderful. Is he a good fucker?"

"Magnificent!"

Her defiance lacked conviction. Paul, however, felt his satisfaction grow. Surely she must have another lover, but she kept returning to him for what he thought was an obvious reason.

"You know, you're a jerk," he said. "The best

fucking you're going to get is right here in this apartment. Now, stand up."

She obeyed, allowing him to turn her around. His hands, buoyed by the suds, skated over her back and buttocks. Paul resembled a father washing his child, his trousers splattered with water, intent and somewhat inexperienced.

Jeanne said, "He's full of mysteries."

That idea vaguely annoyed Paul. He wondered how long he would allow her to go on, and in what way he would bring her down.

"Listen, you dumb dodo," he said. "All the mysteries that you're ever going to find in life are right here."

"He is like everybody." Her voice became dreamy. "But at the same time, he's different."

"Like everybody, but different?" Paul played the game.

"You know, he even frightens me."

"What is he? A local pimp?"

Jeanne laughed in spite of herself. "He could be. He looks it."

She stepped from the tub and wrapped herself in the bulky bath towel. Paul stared at his soapy hands.

"Do you know why I'm in love with him?"

"I can't wait," he said sarcastically.

"Because he knows . . ." She paused, uncertain that she wanted the responsibility. ". . . because he know how to make me fall in love with him."

Paul felt his annoyance bloom into anger. "And you want this man that you love to protect you, and take care of you?"

"Yes."

"You want this gold and shining, powerful warrior to build you a fortress that you can hide in . . ."

He stood up, his voice rising with his height. He looked down at her contemptuously.

". . . so you don't ever have to feel afraid, so you don't have to feel lonely. You don't ever want to feel empty—that's what you want, isn't it?"

"Yes," she said.

"Well, you'll never find him."

"But I have found this man!"

Paul wanted to hit her, to make her see the stupidity of her assertion. He felt a rush of jealousy. She had violated the pact, she had made the outside world seem real for the first time. He had to violate her in some new way.

"Well," he said, "it won't be long until he'll want you to build a fortress for him out of your tits, and out of your cunt, and out of your smile. . . ."

Love was an excuse for feeding upon another for the nourishment of one's own self, Paul thought. The only true way to love was to use another person without making excuses.

"Out of your smile," he continued, "he'll construct some place where he can feel comfortable enough, secure enough, so that he can worship in front of the altar of his own prick. . . ."

Jeanne stood watching him with fascination, the towel wrapped tightly about her. His words frightened her and filled her with fresh desire.

"I have found this man," she repeated.

"No!" he shouted, denying the possibility. "You're alone! You're all alone. And you won't be able to be free of that feeling of being alone until you look death right in the face."

Paul glanced down at the pair of scissors lying on the sink, and his hand moved involuntarily toward them. It would be so easy: her, himself, then nothing but blood. He had been there before, he told himself. He thought of Rosa's body being trundled up the stairs by a pair of ghouls from the autopsist's. A wave of nausea swept over him.

"I know this sounds like bullshit," he said, "some romantic crap. But when you go right up into the ass of death—right up his ass—and feel the womb of fear, then maybe, just maybe you'll be able to find him."

"But I've already found him," Jeanne said, and her voice was unsteady. "He's you. You're that man!"

Paul shuddered and braced himself against the wall. She had tricked him; she had taken too great a chance. All the time she had been talking about him. He had to pay her back. He would show her what despair was.

"Give me the scissors," he said.

"What?" Jeanne was afraid.

"Give me the fingernail scissors."

She picked them up from the sink and passed them to him. Paul caught her by the wrist, and held her hand up to her face.

"I want you to cut the fingernails on your right hand," he told her, but she just looked at him in bafflement.

"These two," he added, pointing. Jeanne took the scissors and carefully trimmed the nails on her middle finger and her forefinger. She replaced the scissors on the edge of the sink rather than offering them to Paul. He began to unfasten his trousers, his eyes never leaving hers. The trousers and his underpants fell about his ankles, revealing his genitals and his muscular, hairy thighs. Paul abruptly turned his back on her and placed both hands on the wall above the toilet.

"Now," he said, "I want you to put your fingers up my ass."

"*Quoi?*" Jeanne couldn't believe what she had heard.

"Put your fingers up my ass! Are you deaf?"

Tentatively she began to explore him. She marveled at his ability to shock her, to push her beyond anything she had imagined. She knew now that the affair could end horribly, in some random act of violence, but she was no longer afraid. Something in the depths of his revealed despair moved her and excited her, carrying her with him. She was willing, even if it meant pushing him farther toward his own disintegration.

She paused, afraid that she was hurting him.

"Go on!" he commanded, and she thrust her fingers deeper.

Paul felt the searing pain. She had passed the first test. He pushed her farther.

"I'm going to get a pig," he told her, gasping, "and I'm going to have that pig fuck you. And I want the pig to vomit in your face. And I want you to swallow the vomit. Are you going to do that for me?"

"Yes," Jeanne said, feeling the momentum of his breathing. She closed her eyes and probed deeper. She began to cry.

"What?"

"Yes!" she answered, going with him now, her head resting against his broad back. There was no escaping. The room held them like a cell, turned them inward on their own passion and degradation. She shared his extreme and lonely ground gatefully: she would agree to anything, do anything.

"And I want the pig to die," Paul went on, breathing heavier, his eyes clamped shut, his face raised in what might have been a benediction. They labored as closely together as they ever had.

"I want the pig to die while you're fucking him. And then you have to go behind, and I want you to smell the dying farts of the pig. Are you going to do all that for me?"

"Yes," she cried, her other arm about his neck,

her face pressed between his shoulders. "Yes, and more than that. And worse, worse than before, much worse. . . ."

Paul came. She had opened herself completely and proved her love. There was no place else to go.

# Chapter Nineteen

I T WAS late, and the hush that had settled in the hotel corridors was disturbed only by the sound of slow, steady footsteps. Paul turned from the stairs and entered a narrow hallway. He felt that he was the guardian of a labyrinth, turning corners, moving in and out of shadows, without will or purpose. He paused in a corner of darkness and listened: there was no sound other than his breathing. He raised a corner of the wallpaper, revealing a peephole, and he put his eye to it and saw the prostitute asleep in her room, alone in a mass of covers, one white leg thrust into view, dark mascara sealing her eyes shut.

Paul moved on. He opened the linen closet at the end of the corridor, which provided a secret view of the Algerian couple on one side, and the American deserter on the other. The bodies were lost in sleep, seemed to fall apart in unconsciousness, their eyelids to be made of soft stone. He moved on to other peepholes, hidden in innocent-looking designs on the wallpaper, in corners and crevices. The hotel reminded him of a spider's web where nothing was secret, nothing inviolate. He checked on all his slumbering guests, but it wasn't people he saw, only slack mouths in uncontrolled grimaces, parched lips of bodies that seemed the negation of flesh. He heard only rasping breath and an occasional invocation called out in sleep. Paul felt he was identifying bodies on slabs in the morgue.

Paul took out a key and unlocked the door of Rosa's room. The odor of flowers was immediate and overwhelming. The lamp on the bedside table remained lit. Her body lay on a bier of sickly, sweet-scented flowers. She wore what looked like a wedding gown, complete with fine white lace and a veil. Her blond hair had been carefully set, and her cheeks and lips heavily rouged. False eyelashes gave her in death the look of someone precisely and demurely asleep. Her slim fingers were folded on her stomach, and the skin of her hands and face had a glossy luminescence. Only her expression was right—a barely perceptible and ironic smile.

Paul sat heavily on the bedside chair and fished the last cigarette from a package of Gauloises. He crumpled the paper and tossed it aside, and lit his cigarette without satisfaction.

"I just made the rounds," he said, without look-ing at Rosa. The door was locked, and it gave him some pleasure to speak to his dead wife. It was a way of ordering his own mind. "I haven't done it for a long time. Everything's fine, calm. The walls are like Swiss cheese in this place."

He looked around, at the walls and ceiling of the sad little room, trying to hold back his anger and grief. Finally he confronted her face.

"You look ridiculous in that makeup," he said. "Like the caricature of a whore—a little touch of Mommy in the night. Fake Ophelia drowned in the bathtub."

He shook his head. His attempted chuckle sounded more like a gasp. Rosa was so still, so final.

"I wish you could see yourself. You'd really laugh."

That was one thing Rosa had, a sense of humor. Distorted humor, maybe, and occasionally cruel, but she could laugh. It seemed irreverent to dress her up like that, and false. The truth was that Paul couldn't say he would have recognized such a woman on the street as his wife.

"You're your mother's masterpiece," he said bitterly, fanning the smoke from before his face. "Christ, there are too many fucking flowers in this place. I can't breathe."

There were even tiny flowers set in her hair. He ground out his cigarette on the rug, beneath his heel. There were some things he had to say, or he knew he would go mad.

"You know, on top of the closet, in that cardboard valise, I found all your little goodies. Pens, key chains, foreign money, French ticklers—the whole lot. Even a clergyman's collar. I didn't know you liked to collect all those little knickknacks the guests left behind. . . ."

There were many things he didn't know, and would never know. It seemed so unfair, and so hopeless.

"Even if the husband lives two hundred fucking years," he said, in sorrow and anger, "he's never going to be able to discover his wife's true nature. I mean, I might be able to comprehend the universe, but I'll never discover the truth about you—never. I mean, who the hell were you?"

For an instant he actually expected Rosa to respond. He waited, listening to the vast silence of the hotel. It was the middle of the night all over the world, everywhere. Paul felt he was the only thing awake in the universe.

"Remember that day," he asked, trying to smile, "the first day I was here? I knew that I couldn't get into your pants unless I said . . ."

He paused, trying to recall their first meeting five years ago. Rosa seemed so proper, so distant, and yet he knew. He was proud, because he thought he had really made a conquest, that they understood each other.

"What did I say? Oh, yes, 'May I have my bill, please? I have to leave.' Remember?"

This time his laugh was genuine. Yes, Rosa had fallen for that ploy, she was afraid he might escape, when he had no intention of leaving. The hotel was cleaner then, and he remembered that he had chosen it for that reason. How oddly things turned out.

Paul felt a sudden need to confess. "Last night I ripped off the lights on your mother, and the whole joint went bananas. All your . . . your guests, as you call them. I guess that includes me, doesn't it?" The anger returned. "It does include me, doesn't it? For five years I was more of a guest in this fucking flophouse than a husband. With privileges, of course. And then, to help me understand, you let me inherit Marcel. The husband's double, whose room was the double of ours."

He felt jealous, genuinely jealous, not for what she and Marcel did together, but because he did not know what they did. There were certain things he was entitled to as a husband, even if just a titular one. She should have told him before dispatching herself—a simple courtesy. But of course he was also afraid to know.

"And you know what?" he said. "I didn't even have the guts to ask him if the same numbers that you and I did were the same numbers you did with him. Our marriage was nothing more than a foxhole for you. And all it took for you to get out was a thirty-five-cent razor and a tub full of water. . . ."

Paul staggered to his feet. He felt a wave of sorrow and rage and frustration break over him. She had no right to leave him like that; her departure was worse than an obscene joke, and one played at his expense.

"You cheap, goddamn, fucking, God-forsaken whore!" He spat out the words, upsetting some of the flowers as he moved closer to the bed. "I hope you rot in hell! You're worse than the dirtiest street pig that anybody could ever find, anywhere. And you know why? Because you lied. You lied to me, and I trusted you. You lied! You knew you were lying."

His hands were deep in his jacket pockets, and his fingers touched something unfamiliar. Slowly he drew out a small photograph. Paul held it up to the light. It was the photo of Jeanne, her full breasts bared to the camera. Paul stared at the photograph as if he didn't recognize her. She must have slipped it into his pocket earlier, he thought. They were all the same, he told himself, tearing the photograph into tiny pieces and scattering them among the flowers. He must live, and that was something else Rosa hadn't understood, or cared about.

"Go on, tell me you didn't lie." He moved his face close to Rosa's, caught a slight medicinal odor amidst that of the flowers. "Haven't you got anything to say about that? You can think up something, can't you? Go on, tell me. Go on, smile, you cunt."

He watched her lips expectantly. They seemed to be made of tallow.

"Go on," he encouraged, "tell me something sweet. Smile at me, and say I just misunderstood."

Tears collected in Paul's eyes and began to trail down his cheeks. He passed the back of his hand across his face, then leaned closer to the body. He wasn't giving up so easily.

"Go on, tell me, you pig-fucker! You goddamn fucking pig-fucking liar!"

He began to sob, his body wracked by heaves. He braced himself against the chair, and reached out to touch her face. It was cold and unyielding. He began to pluck the blossoms from her hair and drop them on the floor about his feet.

"I'm sorry," he said, sniffling, "but I just can't stand it—seeing these goddamn leaves in your face. You never wore makeup—all this fucking shit. . . ."

As delicately as possible, he pulled the false eyelashes away and discarded them. But the effect was still phony and out of character. Paul moved to the sink, where he wet his handkerchief beneath the faucet. Then he began to wipe away the powder and rouge from Rosa's face.

"I'm going to take this lipstick off your mouth. I'm sorry, but I have to."

He stepped back, and looked down at her again. He felt affection, and a compelling need to explain his despair.

"I don't know why you did it," he began. "I'd do it, too, if I knew how. I just don't know."

He paused, and considered suicide. Perhaps he was not the type, but neither was Rosa. Paul spoke to himself: "I have to find a way."

Paul knelt beside the bed and rested his head and arm on Rosa's body. He was about to speak

again, to lose himself in the wash of his own sentimentality. He had never loved Rosa as much in life
as he did in death; he had never been able to see the
value of things and people until they were gone.
This realization didn't make his pain any less. For
once he was stranded without even his own bitter
sense of the absurd.

Someone was pounding on the front door. The
blow echoed through the hotel like the approach
of doom, and for a moment he was afraid. Then the
bell began to ring—a brittle, insistent sound.

He half-called, half-mumbled, "What? All right,
I'm coming," and stumbled to his feet. He turned
back to look at Rosa, and he felt only affection, for
it seemed that he had made some tentative arrange-
ment with his memory of her.

"I have to go, sweetheart," he said. "Baby, someone's calling me."

He smiled down at her frozen features a last time,
and then stepped into the hall, locking the door behind him.

A muffled woman's voice carried up from the
street. "Hello. Is anyone there?"

Paul felt that he had just wakened from a deep
sleep. "I'm coming," he called thickly, and made his
way down the stairs to the lobby.

Two shadows stood massed against the frosted
glass. Paul didn't turn on the light in the foyer, but
went directly to the door. A man and a woman
stood huddled together on the threshold of the
hotel. He couldn't make out their faces.

"Hurry up!" the woman called, catching a glimpse of Paul in the glow from the streetlight, but he didn't move to unlock the door.

"Wake up!" the woman said, knocking loudly, then pressing her face against the glass. "Open the door!"

"It's late," Paul told her. "It's four A.M."

He didn't recognize the woman's voice or the heavily made-up eye that peered in at him.

"I need the usual room," she said. "Number Four. Half an hour will do, or maybe an hour at the most."

Paul shook his head. Why, he wondered, was this woman bothering him? She seemed familiar with the hotel.

"No, indeed," she insisted. "When you're full, you put out a sign. I know. I'm tired of arguing. Call the owner. Move it! The owner's always been helpful to me."

Paul unlocked the door and opened it slightly. He saw a heavy, middle-aged prostitute with blue wings of makeup over her eyes. Behind her stood a man in an overcoat, looking anxiously up and down the street, afraid of being seen.

"Rosa and me, we're old friends," the woman said. "Now, open up. Let me in, if you don't want me to tell her."

While she spoke, the man backed cautiously away, and then turned and walked away without the woman seeing. Paul opened the door for her, and she pushed her way inside quickly.

"Everything's fine," she said, turning. *"Entre."*

She saw the man was gone, and turned angrily on Paul. "Are you happy? He left me."

"I'm sorry," Paul said. He felt that he was participating in a dream, that he and the others weren't real. The possibility that he might have slighted one of Rosa's friends filled him with more sentimental remorse. The woman seemed to want something of him, but he didn't understand exactly what, even as she pushed him toward the door.

"Hurry up and catch him," she said, bringing her face close to his. Paul couldn't see her clearly, but he smelled the stale, sweet odor like that of wilted flowers. "He can't have gone far. Bring him back here. Tell him that it's all right."

Paul dashed out into the street. The light of dawn was just breaking, and he felt tired and confused. Perhaps he should do what the woman asked. The man must have agreed to go with her, he thought. It was only fair that he come back, and that Paul help convince him.

He trotted up the street, the cold morning air filling his lungs. Just moments before he had been mourning his wife, and now he was running an errand for a whore, pimping for his dead wife's memory. The remorse he felt began to drain away, and he felt the stirrings of the old anger. Perhaps this was another of Rosa's jokes, which seemed to lurk for him wherever he turned. He wondered vaguely why it was that prostitutes were so fond of Rosa.

The man in the dark overcoat was nowhere in sight. Paul stopped to catch his breath. He stood listening to the sound of trucks carrying produce through the narrow streets, smelling the damp odor of garbage set in the alley next to him. He felt he was living the ultimate indignity, and there was no one to blame, not even himself. That would have at least been some satisfaction, some way to placate his rage.

He clenched his fists and turned back toward the hotel, the prostitute forgotten. But then in the alley he saw the man in the overcoat, trying to hide in a darkened doorway. His cowardice disgusted Paul. Why had this man agreed to go with the woman, and then refused, causing Paul trouble?

"So you've found me," the man said, trying to laugh. He was thin and delicate-looking, with a melodious, actor's voice. "Please, don't tell her that you found me. Did you see how ugly she is?"

He backed away from Paul, his hands outstretched beseechingly.

"Once my wife was enough for me," he said, "but now she's got a disease that gives her skin like a snake. Put yourself in my place."

Paul took him by the arm. "Come on," he said. Somehow the man's story further enraged him.

"I was drunk," he pleaded. "I took the first one I could find, then we had to walk a bit, and I sobered up . . ."

He tried to pull away, and with sudden, unreasonable fury Paul slammed him with brute force against the metal door of the butcher's shop. He fell in the filthy street and began to crawl backward to escape Paul.

"Leave me alone!" he cried. "You're crazy! Leave me alone!"

He tried to stand and Paul kicked him, propelling him forward across the slick cobblestones.

"Now get the fuck out of here," Paul said. "Faggot!"

The man ran on, limping slightly, glancing in terror over his shoulder.

Paul returned slowly to the hotel, exhausted. How quickly he had descended from the adoration of his wife to the sordid mechanics of his everyday existence.

The woman was waiting in the foyer, seated on the bench and smoking a cigarette. The bright red coal glowed in the shadows.

"I knew it," she said. "You couldn't get him back. Where am I going to find another one at this hour?"

"How much did I make you lose?" He began to search his pockets.

The woman laughed. "Give me what you can. I don't do it for the money. I like it, understand? I do it because I like men."

She put her hand on Paul's.

"You know, you're cute," she said huskily. "If you want, we can do it here. I'm wearing a practical dress, with a first-rate zipper. It opens all the way—I don't even need to take it off. Come on, don't be shy."

She leaned forward into the light, and Paul saw what he thought was a death mask. He drew back, dazed and afraid, and began to move away from her.

"Don't look at me like that!" She stepped to the door. Before going out, she said, "I'm not young anymore. So what? Your wife will be just like me one day."

# *Chapter Twenty*

JEANNE wondered if Paul would be waiting, and what lay in store for her as she ascended in the elevator for what she thought would be the last time. It seemed to her that there was nothing more to gain, that they had passed the last frontier together. But for her the adventure continued, though she knew that its dangers had somehow increased.

She stepped out of the cage and unlocked the door with her own key. She wondered if Paul had discovered the photograph she had dropped into the pocket of his jacket. It was her way of making him think about her, and she liked to think of him looking at it over his morning coffee, or while involved in the mysterious activities of his private life.

The memory of the dead rat returned, and she opened the door cautiously. Silence greeted her, and the glow of sunlight against the circular wall. She caught her breath at the sight of the empty rooms. The furniture was gone. She moved quickly from room to room, confirming what she had difficulty believing, but the apartment looked just as it had that first day. Even the mattress was gone. The walls seemed barer than before, the dark impressions left by paintings more forlorn. Only the odor of their encounters remained, and already that was becoming part of the larger redolence of decline.

She ran out, leaving the door open behind her, and rode the elevator back down into the gloomy foyer. The concierge's window stood open, and Jeanne could see the woman's broad back as she bent over her obscure pastimes. Jeanne stepped up behind her and loudly cleared her throat, but the woman remained oblivious. She hummed an aria from Verdi. It sounded more like an extended moan.

"Excuse me," Jeanne said, "do you remember the man in Number Four?" Jeanne's words seemed to echo through the building, and she remembered the first day she had come, and the frustration she felt trying to gain entrance. The black woman still held her secrets, and she shook her head without even turning around.

"He's been living here for several days," Jeanne prompted.

"I don't know anyone, I tell you," the woman said. "They rent, they sublet. The man in Number Four, the woman in Number One. What do I know?"

Jeanne couldn't believe that Paul had simply moved out. She had expected some surprise, but of course not this one.

"And the furniture," she said. "Where'd he take it? The apartment is empty."

The woman laughed derisively, as if she had heard it too many times before.

"Where do you send his mail?" Jeanne asked. "Give me the address."

"I don't have his address. I don't know anyone."

She was incredulous. "Not even his name?"

"Nothing, *mam'zelle*." She turned her head, hostile now. Jeanne was pushing the guardian of this netherworld too far. After all, Jeanne had entered at her own risk, and she ran toward the door with the enthusiasm of a new idea. If he had left, then the apartment was free once again. It would be a kind of vengeance, she thought, walking down the pavement toward the café, and one that he deserved. He could have told her he was leaving, he could at least have left a message. It seemed impossible that she would never see him again, but she realized— quite suddenly—that she never would.

Her enthusiasm had waned by the time she reached the telephone. She dialed Tom's number.

"I've found an apartment for us," she told him. "Number Three, on the Rue Jules Verne. . . .

Come right away. You understand where it is? . . . I'll wait for you on the fifth floor."

She returned and waited in the foyer until she heard the clamor of Tom and his crew packing into the elevator. Those who couldn't fit raced up the stairs, laughing and shouting at the passengers inside. The whole building seemed transformed by the noise and the sudden effusion of life. She welcomed them in with a smile and a bow.

"You like our apartment?" she asked Tom as he swept in followed by the crew and their jumble of equipment. The cameraman immediately began to set the Arriflex up in the circular room, and Jeanne felt a slight pang of regret, but that was soon forgotten. Tom moved through the empty rooms like an emperor.

"Are you happy?" he asked her, in passing. The cameraman began to film, oblivious of his surroundings. "There's lots of light," Tom added, without waiting for an answer.

Jeanne led him to the small room. "This one's too little for a big bed, but maybe it's all right for a baby. Fidel—that would be a nice name for a kid. Like Fidel Castro."

"But I want a daughter, too," Tom said, and she felt a sudden rush of affection for him. He was so understanding, no matter what she did. . . . She thought of Paul again and missed the urgency the rooms had once contained. Jeanne felt a sense of complacency unknown before to her in that apartment. For the first time she could imagine some family living there—their games and their quarrels and their petty advances. She felt infinitely sad.

"Rosa," said Tom, ignorant of her conflicting emotions. "Like Rosa Luxembourg. She's not as well known, but she wasn't bad in her time. What's the matter?"

"Nothing."

"Good. Then I'll ask some questions for the film. Let's talk about something that interests everybody —sex."

Tom had planned to shock her with that line, while the camera focused upon her, but she was obviously bored and disappointed. He turned to the crew and said, "Cut! It's not possible, no more shooting."

They began to gather up their equipment. Without another word, Tom ushered them out. The script girl waved shyly to Jeanne as she followed the others onto the landing and shut the door softly behind her.

"I wanted to film you every day," Tom said humbly. "In the morning when you wake up, then when you fall asleep. When you smile the first time. . . . And I didn't film anything."

Jeanne turned and moved away from him through the vast, empty rooms. Tom followed, gazing doubtfully at the pile of old furniture draped in the sheet, the cracks and water marks on the walls, the broken molding.

"Today we stopped shooting," he said. "The film is finished."

Jeanne was touched by remorse. "I don't like things that finish."

"One must begin something else right away." Tom turned around in the circular room, to which he had returned, his hands raised in appreciation. "But it's huge."

"Where are you?" called Jeanne from the small room. She moved reluctantly back toward the arena.

"I'm here," he said. "It's too large. You could get lost."

"Oh, stop it." Jeanne didn't feel equal to his enthusiasm. "Now, don't start . . ."

"How did you find this apartment?"

"By chance," she said irritably.

"We'll change everything!"

His words had a certain appeal to her. Was it really possible to change anything? "Everything," she said. "We'll change chance to fate."

Tom ran toward the adjoining room, his arms outspread. "Come on, Jeanne!" he called. "Take off! You're in heaven. Dive, make three turns, descend. What's happening to me? An air pocket?"

He leaned comically against the wall, where his flight had taken him.

"What's happening?" Jeanne asked, laughing in spite of herself.

"Enough of these turbulent zones. We can't act like this," he added, serious. "We can't joke like children—we're adults."

"Adults? But that's terrible."

"Yes, it is terrible."

"Then how must we act?"

"I don't know," he admitted. "Invent gestures, words. For example, one thing I do know, adults are serious, logical, circumspect, hairy . . ."

"Oh, yes," said Jeanne, remembering Paul again. "They face all problems."

Tom knelt on the floor and took Jeanne's hand in his, pulling her down to him.

"I think I understand you," he said softly. "You want a lover more than you want a husband. You know, I could propose something different. You marry who you want, and I'll be the one who carries you away with passion. The lover."

He smiled at her affectionately. Jeanne lay down on the floor and began to pull him toward her.

"Come on," she coaxed. "This is our home now."

But Tom resisted. Jeanne's willingness he found slightly annoying, since he didn't like making love in strange rooms. He wasn't prepared, he told himself. Besides, the room had an unpleasant odor he couldn't quite identify. He stood and zipped up his leather jacket.

"This apartment is not for us," he said. "Absolutely not."

He turned toward the door, leaving her to stand unassisted. He felt claustrophobic and wanted to get out.

"Where are you going?" she asked.

"To look for another apartment."

"Another like what?" She marveled at his instincts.

"One we can live in."

"But we can live here."

"I find this place sad," he said. "It smells. Are you coming with me?"

Jeanne was reluctant to leave. She listened to his jaunty footsteps going down the hall. How different they sounded from the methodical progress of Paul.

"I have to close the windows," she said, "and give back the keys, and make sure everything is in order."

"All right," he called. "I'll see you later."

They said good-bye simultaneously, and then she heard him going quickly down the stairs. Jeanne walked slowly to the window and began to pull down the shutters. She turned and surveyed the room. The shadows had taken over, reducing the golden-red glow of the walls to smoldering brown. The cracks seemed larger and more threatening of collapse, the smell was definitely one of decay.

She walked along the corridor. The small room had lost its charm, and seemed cramped and airless, unsuitable for a child or anyone else. She swung open the door into the bathroom, and felt a chill, in spite of the light from the window above the tub. The sinks were dirty, and for the first time she noticed that chips of gilt were falling from the mirror frame, dusting the cold tile floor with faded gold.

Jeanne felt a sudden, powerful urge to leave. Something threatened her there, and she turned and ran back down the corridor and into the hall. She flung open the door, stepped out onto the landing, and then shut it again without even a last look.

It seemed like an eternity since she had first come

to that dank building. The concierge's window was still open when she stepped off the elevator, but the woman had disappeared. Jeanne was shocked by the idea that she could actually move—she seemed so obese; Jeanne left the key on the counter. It never occurred to her to leave a note. As she was going out, she heard the door next to the elevator open, and glanced back, to see the emaciated hand place another empty bottle on the tiles.

The Rue Jules Verne was unchanged. Workers had never once mounted the scaffolding, the cars seemed permanently parked, the street clean and devoid of people. She hurried past the café and crossed the street, leaving the familiar scene behind. A great feeling of relief came over her, mixed with sadness. She wanted only to get away.

The elevated railway bridge stood before her, and above spread the limpid blue winter sky. Sunlight patterned the walkway of the bridge. With her hands deep in the pockets of her suede coat, and her head down, Jeanne began to cross the Seine, without thinking what might lie ahead.

# Chapter
# Twenty-one

PAUL HAD buried his wife, and removed the furniture from the apartment on the Rue Jules Verne, and he felt cleansed. For the first time since Rosa's suicide, that fact did not weigh heavily on his mind. In fact, he experienced a lightness of spirit and a grudging optimism that he hadn't known in years. The crazy angles of the Paris skyline, the bone-white branches of the sycamores lining the Seine, the rhythm of the passing Métro, the freshness of the breeze—all these seemed pleasant and unique things to be appreciated, things that could matter in his own life. And the sight of a girl in a white maxicoat, her face downturned and set in white fox fur, moving toward him with measured steps, was an affirmation that couldn't be denied.

Jeanne was oblivious of her surroundings, except that the clash of the passing train and the people about her constituted minor irritations. She thought of nothing but the blandness of her own life, and the futility of human relationships. The man who stopped beside her, turned, and fell into step with her, was simply an inconvenience to be ignored. For a few moments they matched each other stride for stride; then he moved slightly ahead of her, and she was forced to look at him.

"It's me again," Paul said lightly, one hand raised in greeting.

She slowed down, but didn't stop. She was surprised by the elegance of his appearance. He wore a tailored navy blazer, complemented by a peppermint-striped shirt, and a wide silk tie. He was even dapper, and his gait reflected his confidence. She no longer trusted him.

"It's over," she said.

"It's over," he agreed, shrugging his shoulders and skipping to keep up with her. "Then it begins again."

"What begins again?" she looked at him, and thought he seemed more open, and consequently vulnerable. It was as if away from that apartment he had shed some protective armor, like a molting animal emerging from its lair. Jeanne, however, felt reserved in the open. The apartment had been its own defense and hers, but in the harsh light of the world she wanted to keep her own secrets.

"I don't understand anything anymore," she said, walking faster.

He took her arm and guided her toward the steps to the Métro platform. She held her body rigid, unused to his insistent pursuit—that was certainly something new, she thought. Paul paused in the shadow of the doorway and touched her cheek, and Jeanne relaxed. She knew it was hopeless, but she couldn't just leave him.

"Well, there's nothing to understand," Paul said, and before she could answer, he kissed her softly on the lips. He felt her warmth and the reality of her flesh: she was a woman to him now, and an attractive one. For her, it was the first tender embrace of his she could remember.

They walked along the Métro platform, arm-in-arm, resembling a moody young niece and a kindly uncle exchanging confidences.

"We left the apartment," Paul explained, "and now we meet again, with love and all the rest of it."

He smiled at her, but Jeanne shook her head.

"The rest?" she asked.

Before he could answer, the Métro pulled in, and they boarded it on impulse, Paul pulling her along and guiding her to an empty seat. They sat close together now, like lovers.

"Listen," he said, happy to be able to talk about himself, and free of his grief. "I'm forty-five. I'm a widower. I've got a little hotel that's kind of a dump, but it's not completely a flophouse. And I used to live on my luck, but then I got married. My wife killed herself . . ."

The train screeched to a halt. A crowd moved toward the doors, slamming them open. Paul and Jeanne looked at each other, and suddenly got off again. She realized that she didn't want to hear about his life, which seemed sad and slightly sordid. In silence they climbed the concrete steps into the orderly, expansive neighborhood of the Étoile, bathed in sunlight.

"What do we do now?" Jeanne asked.

"You told me you were in love with a man, and that you wanted to live with him. I'm the one you love. So we live together. We'll be happy, we'll even get married, if you want. . . ."

"No," she said, tired of their rambling. "What do we do now?"

"Now we're going to have a little drink. We're going to celebrate, be gay."

Paul believed what he was saying, but he felt uncertain as to how to entertain a young woman in the afternoon. Not that it mattered. If she loved him, they would be content wherever they stopped. The idea of formally courting her appealed to him. He needed to have fun, and to convince her that he was capable of it.

"What the hell," he said, "I'm no prize. I picked up a nail when I was in Cuba in 1948, and now I've got a prostate like an Idaho potato. But I'm still a good stick man, even if I can't have any children."

Jeanne felt confused. She was still attracted to him by the memory of the affair, but put off by a vague and rising distaste. She felt exposed in the bright winter sun.

"Let's see," Paul said, searching for something else to tell her. "I don't have any stamping grounds, I don't have any friends. I suppose if I hadn't met you, I'd probably settle for a hard chair and a hemorrhoid."

She wondered why his allusions were always so anal. He held onto the cuff of her coat as he stopped on the pavement, and reared back to look into the Salle Wagram, a dance hall sometimes used for minor boxing matches. The sound of orchestra music reached them, but from the street the hall looked empty.

"And to make a long, dull story even duller," Paul continued, leading her toward the Salle, "I come from a time when a guy like me would drop into a joint like this, to pick up a young chick like you. In those days we'd call her a bimbo."

They entered arm-in-arm. The hall resounded with the music of a small but ardent orchestra. The setting was more like the interior of a barn, with a vast dome for a ceiling, and garishly lit by dozens of hanging globes. Various tiers of tables overlooked the main floor. There a dance contest was in progress. Several dozen couples wearing clothes that had been fashionable fifteen years before moved in a strange, rhythmic pattern that Jeanne had never seen before. The men had long Valentino sideburns, and the women's lacquered hair glistened. They reminded her of vain, colorful birds prancing in a cage, under the eyes of severe middle-aged men and women who sat at a long wooden table on one side of the floor. Before these seated observers were spread paper and pencils. Numbers printed on large squares of cardboard were pinned to the backs of each contestant, and as they twirled, the judges craned their necks. A few waiters stood watching, but most of the hall was empty. White tablecloths had been spread over the tables around the actual dance floor, but the tables on the other tiers supported upturned chairs by the hundreds. A wooden railing separated the dancers from the empty expanses of the ballroom, now a tango palace.

Paul led Jeanne straight across the floor and up onto the second tier, where a waiter prepared a table for them with surly efficiency. Paul extravagantly ordered champagne, and took his seat across from Jeanne. He knew she would see the humor of it. The two of them were all that mattered, and the absurdity of their surroundings might provide amusement. But Jeanne could only stare at the contestants. They seemed so grotesque, flitting about in the great, gloomy hall, motivated by the beat of the music and the desire to be chosen by a panel of old men and women.

The waiter brought the champagne, poured their glasses full, and left them alone. Jeanne just rested her head on her elbows. Paul moved next to her.

"I'm awfully sorry to intrude," he said, faking a British accent to amuse her, "but I was so struck with your beauty that I thought I would offer you a glass of champagne."

She just looked at him blankly.

"Is this seat taken?" Paul asked, carrying on with the joke, though he knew she didn't care.

"What?" she said. "No, it's not taken."

"May I?"

"If you'd like to."

Paul sat with an extragavant flourish, and lifted her champagne glass to her lips. Jeanne turned her face away. His parody seemed too close to the truth, and they both felt uncomfortable. Paul drank deeply, and poured his glass full again. Things weren't going quite as he had planned.

"You know the tango?" he asked, and Jeanne shook her head. "It's a rite. You understand 'rite'? Well, you must watch the legs of the dancers."

He hailed the waiter and ordered a bottle of Scotch and some glasses. The waiter looked at him for a moment, then tango to get the whiskey. Paul wanted to enjoy himself, to spend money, to celebrate, and he didn't care what anyone else thought, except Jeanne.

"You haven't drunk your champagne," he said. "Now it's warm. I've ordered you a Scotch."

The waiter brought the bottle. He walked back toward the far end of the hall. Their table was isolated. Paul poured the drinks with a heavy hand.

"You're not drinking your Scotch," he gently reprimanded. "Now, come on, just a sip, for Daddy."

He held the glass to her lips. She looked at him sadly, and Paul felt a growing desperation. But then she drank, knowing it would please him, though the whiskey seared her throat.

"Now, if you love me," he coaxed, "you'll drink all of it."

She drank again. "Okay," she said, "I love you." It was just a phrase.

"Bravo!" said Paul.

"Tell me about your wife."

That was the one thing Paul didn't want to talk about. That was past now; he was going to enjoy himself, he was going to begin a new life.

"Let's talk about us," he said.

Jeanne just looked around, at the dancers and judges, and the small clutch of waiters in the shadows. "But this place is so pitiful."

"Yes, but I'm here, aren't I?"

Jeanne said sarcastically, "Monsieur Maître d'Hôtel."

"That's rather nasty."

Paul decided that she was just teasing him. After the intensely passionate encounters they had known, it didn't seem possible that she could mock him. But for her, the more Paul told her about himself, the less attractive he became.

"Anyway, you dummy," he went on, "I love you, and I want to live with you."

"In your flophouse." It was almost a sneer.

"In my flophouse? What the hell does that mean?" Paul was growing angry, and the effect of the whiskey seemed to aggravate it. Jeanne seemed to be missing the point.

"What the hell difference does it make if I have a flophouse or a hotel or a castle?" he shouted. "I love you! What the fuck difference does it make?"

Jeanne moved to the next chair, afraid that he might hit her. She picked up her glass and drank the Scotch off neat. The hall, the dancers, Paul, and even herself depressed her. It was no good going on, but she didn't want to admit it, to Paul or to herself.

Placated by her drinking, Paul tipped up his own glass. Then he refilled them both. The alcohol made him more ardent, and at the same time he felt that quiet desperation mounting. Jeanne stared at the dance floor. The music and the couples pinned with large numerals twirled faster and faster as her own mind became clouded. She wished she hadn't drunk so quickly, though now the Scotch left her thirsty. She watched the dancers' legs. They pranced and jerked their heads mechanically.

Suddenly the music stopped. The dancers turned and swept back to their tables, where they perched on the edges of their chairs with fixed smiles, heads turned toward the judges. A middle-aged woman in a flower print dress of clashing reds and purple, and wire-rimmed spectacles, stood behind the long table and announced in a loud, efficient voice, "The jury has chosen the following best ten couples."

She adjusted her glasses and held a paper up before her. A hush fell over the hall as she began to read off the numbers. One by one the chosen ones swept back onto the floor, strutting and twirling to face one another, primed for the music that was about to begin. Gradually the floor filled with poised couples. They held each other with rigid limbs, and stared into each other's eyes blindly. They reminded Jeanne of mannequins.

The woman in the flower print raised her hands exuberantly and called out, "And now, ladies and gentlemen, good luck on the last tango!" Her words reverberated in the cavernous hall. The final judgment was at hand.

The instant music was loud and melodious and infinitely depressing to Jeanne, who could see the daylight slanting through the doorway. To be drunk in the afternoon, and watching automatons, made her want to cry. Paul sat opposite her, watching the dancers over his shoulder, morose and unpredictable. Once again Jeanne tried to watch the dancers' legs. They moved in perfect unison as each couple dipped and glided, and then bent backward in a stylized flourish, their smiles frigid, their eyes and faces blank. She began to wonder if they were really people. It was impossible to imagine them pursuing ordinary human activities.

"Give me some more whiskey," she told Paul.

"Oh, I thought you weren't drinking."

"I'm thirsty now. I want some more drink."

Paul stood and walked unsteadily around the table. "All right. I think that's a good idea." He carefully poured more Scotch into their glasses.

Jeanne felt dizzy, and she carefully pulled the glass toward her.

"Wait a minute," Paul said before she could drink. He pronounced his words thickly, preparing to make a boast. "Because . . . because you're really beautiful . . ."

Jeanne thought that was the toast, and she drank.

"Wait a minute!" he shouted, slamming his glass on the table. Scotch spilled over his hand and dripped onto the floor.

"Okay."

"I'm sorry, I'm terribly sorry," he said in his British accent. "I didn't mean to spill my drink."

Jeanne raised her own glass. "Well, let's have a toast," she said, "to our life in the hotel!"

"No, fuck all that."

Paul kicked over a chair as he came to sit beside her. He leaned against her heavily, and she noticed the lines about his eyes, and his thinning hair. Everything she had said about him in the apartment the day before had been true. He was an old man, and now he even smelled like one, after he had gotten into the cooking sherry. Jeanne couldn't look at him without thinking of his body. She had never before really thought of his girth, and the wrinkles in his skin. The secret of his name and existence had falsely preserved him for her.

"Come on," Paul said, "let's drink a toast to our life in the country."

"You're a nature-lover? You never told me that."

"Oh, for Christ's sake." Paul knew all they would

do in the country was make love. Why was she taunting him? He added, going along with her mood, "Yeah, I'm nature boy. Can't you see me with the cows? With chicken shit all over me?"

"Oh, sure."

"Why not?" he asked, offended.

"All right, we'll have a house and cows. I will be your cow, too."

"And listen," he said, laughing raucously. "I get to milk you twice a day. How about that?"

"I hate the country," she admitted, thinking of the villa. Everything was becoming obscene, tainted by the alcohol and the sight of those tirelessly twirling bodies drained of life.

"What do you mean you hate the country?" he demanded.

"I hate it."

Jeanne stood up and braced herself against the back of her chair. She felt she had to get out.

"I prefer to go to the hotel," she said, and the idea didn't sound too ridiculous. Maybe there was still a chance, she thought, maybe Paul would look and sound different again, alone with her in a room. Maybe she could forget all this, and what he had told her. "Come on, let's go to the hotel."

But Paul took her hand and led her toward the dance floor. They stumbled down from the raised tier, their feet loud on the bare boards, but the music covered them.

"Let's dance," said Paul.

Jeanne shook her head, but Paul persisted, pulling her toward the main arena. The dancers pretended not to notice them.

"Come on," he cajoled. "Let's dance."

They staggered among the participants. Jeanne felt her legs going. The music and the stale air of the hall seemed to work with the whiskey; then she smelled the reek of a dozen perfumes. The spotlights blinded her, and the other couples whipped past them with stylized grace that made Paul's antics outrageous. He gripped her in the dance pose, then lifted one leg and curled it around behind him, mocking the others. He strutted back and forth, his chin raised theatrically, lifting his knees high and slamming his feet on the floor. He attempted to twirl Jeanne beneath one hand, but she slipped and fell heavily, and slid a few feet across the floor.

"Don't you want to dance?" Paul asked. He began to dance by himself, twisting and dipping among the couples. They never missed a step. It was absurd, and Paul enjoyed it. He felt good, high on the whiskey and the spectacle. His new life was just beginning, and he would live it to the full, the way he wanted. He tried to perform a leap, and fell to his knees.

The woman in the flower print stood at her place, speechless with indignation. The other judges hovered around her, speaking in harsh whispers, but none of them seemed willing to approach the drunken, irreverent couple.

"The floor is already full!" the woman in the

flower print shouted, waving her hands and advancing toward Paul. "You're exaggerating." Like everything else in the event, she took him seriously.

Paul thought that was very funny. He began to laugh, and to dance around her like a matador.

"Get out, sir! What are you doing?"

"Madame!" he said, grabbing the woman about the waist and striking the tango pose. Paul began to move her ponderously around the floor, and she struggled to get free. The judges watched in outrage, while the contestants continued to perform.

"This is not possible," the woman said.

"It's love," Paul said. "Always. *L'amour toujours.*"

"But it's a contest!" She finally pulled herself away. Her colleagues behind the judges' table came cautiously forward.

"Where's love fit in?" the woman shouted. "Go to the movies to see love. Now, go on, get out of here!"

Jeanne took Paul by the arm and pulled him toward the exit. But he stopped at the edge of the floor. As the judges all watched him, he pulled down his trousers, bent over, and thrust out his ass. The spectators gasped.

He and Jeanne stumbled off the floor. They stopped in a darkened corner, amidst upturned tables, and sat heavily against the wall. The music continued, unbroken and indifferent.

"Beauty of mine, sit before me," Paul said, trying to touch Jeanne's cheek, but she turned away. She groaned with real anguish.

*"Garçon!"* Paul snapped his fingers, but no waiter came. They were alone. "Champagne!" he called, and began to move his hands in time with the music. "If music be the food of love, play on!"

He turned to Jeanne and saw that tears were running down her cheeks.

"What's the matter with you?" he asked.

"It's finished."

"What's the matter with you?" he repeated, refusing to understand what she said.

"It's finished."

"What's finished?"

"We're never going to see each other again, never."

"That's ridiculous." Paul waved his hand, dismissing her words. Then he took her hand and pushed it down inside his trousers. He repeated softly, "That's ridiculous."

"It's not a joke." Jeanne took his penis in her fist and began to stroke it. She stared straight ahead, the tears still coursing down her cheeks.

Paul leaned back against the wall. "Oh, you dirty rat," he sighed.

"It's finished."

"Look, when something's finished, it begins again. Don't you see?"

"I'm getting married," Jeanne said mechanically. "I'm going away. It's finished." Her hand moved faster.

"Oh, Jesus!"

Paul climaxed, and Jeanne withdrew her hand in disgust. She had milked him, and the last of his strength drained away. She wiped her hand on his handkerchief.

"Look," he said, trying to joke about her revulsion. "That's not a subway strap, that was my cock."

The music died, and the hall filled with the echo of shuffling feet and the judge's harsh announcement of the contest winners. Jeanne couldn't understand the words, but it didn't matter. She saw the scene—and she and Paul in it. He had become ugly, his life sordid and pointless, his sex useless. She looked at him, and confronted a drunken bum. She loathed him and herself.

"It's finished," she said, and she got up and walked to the door.

"Wait a minute," Paul called. "You dumb bimbo!"

He struggled to his feet and fastened his trousers. By the time he reached the door, Jeanne was already walking quickly toward the main boulevard.

"Shit!" Paul said, blinded by the sudden light, and unsteady on his feet. "Wait a minute, god-damnit!"

He started up the street after her, but Jeanne walked faster. The sound of his feet frightened her.

"Hey, Rube!" he called playfully, but Jeanne didn't turn around. "Come here!"

She crossed the street at the corner, just as the light changed, and Paul had to wait. His anger and his frustration grew. Suddenly he realized that if she left him now, he would never see her again.

"Come here!" he shouted again, stepping out into

the traffic in the blare of horns, and hurrying on. "I'm going to get you, bimbo!"

Then they were both running. They moved in and out of the shadow of sycamore trees lining the pavement, and the flashes of sunlight focused on the contradiction: a pretty young woman with her coat open and her hair flying, pursued by a man old enough to be her father, too short of wind and grace for such a contest. They might have been attached by an invisible cord that grew shorter as she slowed her pace, then lengthened again as she moved away from him. But the invisible cord never broke. They remained partners in a curious ritual, isolated from the world through which they dashed.

It was rush hour, and the Champs Élysées was crowded. Jeanne raced along, dodging in and out of the waves of pedestrians, staying just ahead of Paul. Her fear grew when she realized he was not giving up, and in panic she tried to think of a place she would be safe. She could think only of her mother's apartment, on the Rue Vavin in Montparnasse, and she was certain Paul would not last that long.

He had already fallen behind, and she slowed her pace, watching him over her shoulder. Half a block apart, they passed Grand Palais, splendid in the afternoon sunlight, and the Gare d'Orsay, and crossed the Seine, the sound of their footsteps lost in the growl of competing traffic. Paul stayed with her, though he was gasping for breath, and pains shot through his chest.

At the edge of Montparnasse, Jeanne wheeled on him and screamed, "Stop! Stop!" Then she ran on.

"Hold it!" Paul begged, but it was no use. He lunged forward again.

Jeanne neared her mother's apartment building and slowed. She didn't want Paul to follow her there, and could think of no alternative. She was aware of his heavy footsteps behind her. Finally he caught up, barely able to breathe, and grabbed her by the arm.

"It's finished!" she said, jerking away. "That's enough."

"Hey, cool it."

Paul leaned against the wall and tried to reason with her, but she walked around him. "Stop!" she shouted. "It's finished. Now, go away. Go away!"

Paul loped along behind her, still gasping for breath.

"I can't win," he said. "Give me a break."

He struggled to get ahead of her, and blocked her path. He smiled, desperate to gain control, his hands resting on his hips. He said affectionately, "Hey, dummy . . ."

Jeanne spoke rapidly in French, "This time I'm going to call the police."

He determined then not to let her go. He would do anything to prevent her from getting away from him. She was his last chance for love.

She brushed past him.

"Well, shit, I'm not in your way," he said bitterly. "I mean, *après vous, mademoiselle.*"

She paused on the corner, looking across at the doorway of her mother's apartment building. She was trembling, and trying to control the panic that threatened to drive her straight through the door. Paul saw that she was truly afraid. He could reassure her later, he thought, after he discovered where she lived.

"So long, sister," he said, passing her and stepping into the street. "Besides, you're a crummy-looking broad. I don't care if I never see you again."

He walked on, pretending to have lost interest. Nonchalantly, he placed a stick of chewing gum in his mouth. Jeanne watched him, and then turned and dashed across the street. She slipped through the door of the apartment house, but as she was shutting it, Paul bolted across the street and up the steps, stepped into the foyer just as Jeanne shut the door of the elevator cage. She looked at him in terror as he grasped the frail iron handle and tried to jerk it open.

The elevator moved slowly upward.

"Shit!" Paul said, leaped up the stairs, trying to keep abreast of the machine.

"You're finished!" Jeanne cried out in French. *"Tu as fini!"*

He reached the second landing and grabbed the elevator handle, but he was too late. The cage continued to mount, with Jeanne pressed in the back corner.

*"Les flics . . ."* she stammered.

"Oh, fuck the police."

The elevator passed the third landing before Paul could reach the door. He continued to climb.

*"Tu as fini!"* she shouted down at him.

The cage lunged to a halt on the fourth floor, and Jeanne leaped out onto the landing, began pounding on the door of her mother's apartment. Paul came up behind her.

"Listen," he said, panting, "I want to talk to you."

Jeanne ran past him and began to pound on the other apartment door, but there was no response. Paul followed her, and when he touched her arm, she began to scream.

"Now, this is getting ridiculous," he said.

"Help!" she screamed, searching through her purse for her key. "Help me!"

No one came. She scrabbled at the lock of her mother's door, and when it opened, almost fell inside. Paul was right behind her, blocking the door with his shoulder. She rushed ahead of him through the apartment, seeing nothing, driven by a panic that focused on a single object lying in the bureau drawer. There was no stopping him. She had always known she couldn't hide from him. Still, she was not prepared for his ruthlessness.

"This is the title shot," Paul said, pausing to gaze around at the prints and primitive weapons. "We're going all the way."

Jeanne pulled open the drawer and took out her father's service pistol. It felt heavy, cold, and capable, and she hid it inside her coat before turning to face him.

"I'm a little old," Paul said, smiling sadly. "I'm full of memories now."

Jeanne watched him with horrible fascination as he picked up one of her father's army caps and placed it at an angle on his head. He moved toward her.

"How do you like your hero?" he asked. "Over easy or sunny-side-up?" He was still charming.

He discarded the cap with a flourish. She was there now, she was his now, and he couldn't let her go. The idea that he had at last found someone to love seemed beautiful.

"You ran through Africa and Asia and Indonesia, and now I've found you." Paul meant it. "And I love you," he added.

He stepped close to her, and didn't notice that her coat fell open. The gun barrel turned toward him. He raised his hand to touch her cheek, and whispered, "I want to know your name."

"Jeanne," she said, and pulled the trigger.

The explosion carried him back a few paces, but he didn't go down. The reek of burned cordite filled the air, and the gun in Jeanne's hand trembled. Paul bent slightly forward, clutching his stomach with one hand, the other still raised. His expression had not changed.

"Our children . . ." he began. "Our children . . ."

He turned and staggered to the glass door leading out onto the terrace. As it swung open, the fresh wind caught his hair, and for an instant he seemed almost young. He stepped out onto the tiles, steadied himself against the railing, and turned his face toward the bright blue sky. Paris sprawled before him.

With unhurried grace, he removed the chewing gum from his mouth and delicately pressed it against the underside of the balcony railing.

"Our children," he said, "will remember . . ."

That was the last thing he knew he said. But his final word on earth was murmured in a Tahitian dialect. He collapsed heavily against the base of a potted pine, curled like a child in sleep, and died smiling.

"I don't know who he was," Jeanne repeated to herself, the gun still in her hand, her eyes wide and unseeing. "He followed me, he tried to rape me. He was crazy . . . I don't know his name, I don't know him, I don't know . . . He tried to rape me, he was crazy . . . I don't even know his name."

That part, at least, was true.

From the publisher who brought you
*The Sensuous Woman*
*The Sensuous Man*
and
*The Happy Hooker!*

# SCORING

## by DAN GREENBURG

SCORING is the frankest and funniest sexual memoir written in our time. The title comes from the most popular national pastime where First Base was a goodnight kiss and Home Plate too rarely reached. Dan Greenburg is a compulsive scorekeeper. He keeps a record of every girl he has ever necked with or petted above the waist and every girl he has ever scored with. A harder-working necker, grappler, pincher, petter, and finally, scorer never survived to write about it. SCORING is riotously funny, disarming, candid, touching and true. It is Dan Greenburg's story, but it is yours, too—whether your coming-of-age occurred in the 40s, 50s or 60s. Some things just don't change.

A DELL BOOK $1.50

If you cannot obtain copies of this title at your local bookseller, just send the price (plus 15c per copy for handling and postage) to Dell Books, Post Office Box 1000, Pinebrook, N. J. 07058.

The hottest heist since
*The Anderson Tapes* ...
by the author of
*Miami Golden Boy*.

# MILLIONAIRES

## by HERBERT KASTLE

The place was Bay Island, connected to Florida
by a narrow bridge. On it were twelve luxurious
homes, each one occupied by a millionaire. Even
the President of the United States, a frequent
visitor, was just another guest in the company
of the super-rich.

Walter Danforth "Bucky" Prince came to the
island with a distinguished family name, a repu-
tation as a super-stud and a handpicked crew of
helpers. His purpose was simple: to take over
Bay Island and loot it. . . .

"Steaming sex, violence and suspense!"
*Library Journal*

### A DELL BOOK $1.50

If you cannot obtain copies of this title from your local bookseller, just
send the price (plus 15c per copy for handling and postage) to Dell Books,
Post Office Box 1000, Pinebrook, N. J. 07058.

You saw her on TV.
You read about her in *Time*.
She's front page news coast-to-coast.
She's frank, she's controversial, she's ...

# The Happy Hooker

by Xaviera Hollander
with Robin Moore and Yvonne Dunleavy

And she tells you all about it! Xaviera Hollander is young, beautiful, the most famous and successful madam in New York City. "Mine is not a house of ill repute," she has remarked on national television, "it is a house of pleasure." She made headlines recently when it was learned at the Knapp Commission in New York City that she paid $18,000 for police protection she never received.

Far from the controversial image of a prostitute, Xaviera is well-read, articulate, fluent in a dozen languages, and bursting with *joie de vivre*.

THE HAPPY HOOKER is her remarkable life story.

*An original Dell Book    $1.50*

# How many of these Dell Bestsellers have you read?

If you cannot obtain copies of these titles from your local bookseller, just send the price (plus 15c per copy for handling and postage) to Dell Books, Post Office Box 1000, Pinebrook, N. J. 07058.